DATE MY PROFESSOR

IVY COLLINS

STARWATCH
PRESS

$$1$$

SOPHIE

$\mathcal{N}$othing messes up your ability to focus on complicated data structures quite like being evicted from your apartment in the middle of class.

As my phone starts playing *Jingle Bell Rock*, the other students shoot me death glares. Up front, Professor Elijah Oliver pauses partway through writing out a function on the old-fashioned chalkboard. I cringe as he turns around and fixes his deep green eyes right on me. He quirks one of those sharp blond eyebrows my way, and I squirm in my seat, glancing down at the number on the phone with increasing panic.

"Please, Miss Eddings," Professor Oliver drawls, "don't let me interrupt your eighties Christmas nostalgia with my boring exam review." He says it in that crisp British accent that normally makes me squirm in my chair for entirely different reasons. A few of the college girls behind me titter with laughter on cue.

Professor Oliver has a sharp wit, but it isn't his jokes that make girls laugh; he could probably spend the whole class telling hokey knock-knock jokes and get the exact same reaction. The man is—not to put too fine a point on the matter—absolutely drop-dead gorgeous. His aristocratic features and sharp Oxford button-down shirts stand out like a sore thumb in the middle of our proudly-weird Austin, Texas campus. I have zero doubts that every girl in my class—and some of the guys, probably—have spent a certain portion of the past hour dreaming about running their fingers through his short, messy blond hair and kissing the edges of that wicked smirk that often graces his mouth.

It doesn't hurt matters, of course, that he's also a certified genius. I shudder to think how much money the university must have spent to entice him across an entire ocean. As a leading researcher in artificial intelligence, Professor Elijah Oliver probably doesn't even need to teach boring bachelor's level classes. He runs some kind of crazy start-up incubator for the university and consults for a lot of the high-tech companies in the area. I guess he must like *something* about us moronic students, all the same—because here he is, spending his Wednesday evening making fun of my ringtone.

Normally, I would throw back an equally acid retort —we both relish trading rejoinders—but today, my brain is coming up empty.

"I... I'm sorry," I sputter out, wilting beneath his sharp eyes. "I have to take this, sir. I'll be... I'll be right back." I stumble to my feet, slinking for the door to the hallway, praying to god that I'm about to get the first good news I've had all month.

I try to ignore the way his eyes heat up my back as I creak the door open and leave the classroom.

"Hello?" I ask breathlessly, as I answer in the middle of a jingling note. "This is Sophie."

"*I was under the impression we'd finished our discussion, Miss Eddings,*" says a disapproving male voice on the other end of the line. My heart sinks all the way down into my stomach. "*I want you out of that apartment tonight. I won't ask again. After this, I'm changing the locks.*"

Tears blur at my eyes. "I don't have anywhere to go," I choke. "Please, I just need another week or so to find a place, I've been looking, I *promise*—"

"*That's not my problem,*" my landlord replies curtly. "*I don't want the police showing up at my property ever again, Miss Eddings. If your boyfriend wants to fight with you, he can do it elsewhere.*"

"He's my ex-boyfriend!" I burst out desperately. "And I didn't *invite* him there, I've had to change my phone number and move twice—"

"*Well, now you can move a third time.*" The voice on the other end of the line is hard and unsympathetic. "*Tonight, Miss Eddings. And don't call me again unless it's to tell me you're gone.*"

The line goes dead.

I stare blankly down at my phone for another few minutes, trying to process everything. The reality of my desperate situation refuses to manifest, though. My brain keeps searching for another alternative, another way forward. I'm a computer science student—if anyone knows how to adapt, it should be me. But I've truly, properly exhausted all my options.

My ex-boyfriend Jordan Lynch has been *ex* for more than a year now. He wasn't always terrible—he was once a model high school student, with an open fraternity spot waiting for him and his college career mapped out from start to finish. But Jordan started partying a little too hard with his frat brothers, and it got to the point where I saw him drunk more often than I saw him sober. He got more angry, more threatening. I didn't stick around to see how long it would take before he finally hit me. Instead, I broke it off and begged him to get some help for his problem.

I've spent the last year desperately trying to dodge Jordan while I finish my degree. I can't afford to leave university—I can barely afford to *go* to university, even with my generous scholarship. But Jordan doesn't know how to take no for an answer. He showed up at my apartment in the middle of the night last week, pounding on my door in a drunken fit. My neighbor, understandably terrified, called the police. By the time the authorities arrived, Jordan was gone... but my landlord wasn't pleased to find out that my problems had scared the girl next door.

So now... I'm no longer *his* problem.

"Hey, Jingles," a guy says behind me. "Would you *move* it? You're blocking the door."

I jump out of the way, glancing behind me. Students are filing out of the lecture hall. *Oh god,* I realize. *Class is over?* How long have I been standing here, having my little panic attack?

My breath comes short. My head begins to pound. I don't know what to do. I sink back against the wall, kneading my palms into my eyes, trying desperately not to cry. It's a losing battle. There are hot tears leaking out of the corners of my eyes.

Before I know it, I'm sitting against the wall, hiding my face against the torn-up knees of my jeans.

"Miss Eddings?"

Oh, god.

It's Professor Oliver's voice. I can feel him standing over me in the hallway. There's a suspicious curiosity in the accented way that he says my name. He knows something is terribly wrong, but he's too polite to make a fuss about it right away.

I try to reply—but I have to choke down a sob first, and I know he hears it. "I... I'm sorry," I manage. "I left my things in the hall. I think I n-need to go get them."

He sighs heavily, as though put-upon. Warm hands slide beneath my arms, hauling me up from the tile floor. I'm forced to look up at him in bewilderment as he curls his arm around my back, holding me up against him.

Even in the midst of an absolute panic attack, I'm capable of appreciating the rare, guilty pleasure of the moment. Every girl in my class would die to be in my position right now, pressed up next to our wicked British professor, feeling the heat of his body against mine. He's taller than I realized—a full head and a half taller than me —but he's looking down at me such that there's not much distance at all between his face and mine. Those dark green eyes are even more intense up close like this, and oh my *god*, he's wearing some kind of sharp cologne that hits me like a drug. I fit against his side like I was made for him. The crazy thought won't let me be, though maybe it's just because my blood is up and my head is a panicked mess.

His eyes darken as he looks down at me, and his fingers tighten around my side, tickling against my rib. I wonder if I'm imagining the heat that flickers through his touch—but it's gone an instant later, buried beneath that proper British concern. "Come on inside," he says. "Unless you'd *prefer* to cry in the hallway?"

"Who... who's interrupting who, now?" I retort weakly. I want it to be a kind of challenge—a way to re-establish normalcy between us—but my voice trembles on the words.

"How rude," Professor Oliver replies idly. He's playing along with my pathetic attempt, at least. "You left your things in the lecture hall. If anything, you're preventing me from closing up and going home on time." His hand tightens again on my side, oddly reassuring. He opens the door for both of us and pulls me safely inside, out of view. "I hope you intend to apologize for the trouble."

The door closes behind us with a hard *snap*, and I break out into laughing, mortified sobs.

ELIJAH

I have never seen Sophia Eddings speechless before.

The moment she fails to reply to my needling about her phone, I know that something is incredibly wrong. Sophie keeps her composure very well—I don't think there's anything terribly revealing on her face—but something subtle about her behavior as she flees my class rings alarm bells in my mind. I have to resist the immediate urge to go after her, with more than forty students staring at me, waiting for me to finish the function on the blackboard. But her things are still in her seat, and I reassure myself that she'll have to return for them, one way or another.

My mind, I'm afraid, is not on the exam review. I rush through the last few bullet points on my list, dimly aware of the growing worry in my students' eyes as I do so. "Wait!" gasps a boy near the back of the class, as I adjourn for the evening fifteen minutes early. "Can you please go back to the different sorting algorithms, sir—"

"I went over sorting algorithms for two whole weeks, Mister O'Dell," I inform him, with a forced cheer in my voice. I start packing up my things, clearly signalling to the stragglers that I have no interest in taking further questions. "You might not recall, as you slept through half of it. Given your confident naps, I will refer you to my esteemed colleague, Professor Wikipedia. His office hours are twenty-four seven, and I believe he can accommodate your eccentric sleeping schedule."

Two of the girls giggle at that, and I have to resist the urge to snap at them. There's little I find more irritating than those who laugh at others' misfortune. If you're going to poke fun at someone, damn it all, you ought to at least exercise your *words* instead of making mindless tittering noises. Laughter is just so... *lazy*.

"I'll see you at the exam in two days," I tell them. The two girls blink at me in bewilderment, and I wonder if some of my irritation has seeped into my voice. I push away the thought and start shooing students out the door.

Sophie's bag is still draped over her seat.

I mutter something very unprofessional under my breath and stalk for the door outside.

I nearly miss her on my way out. She's curled up against the wall, with her head on her knees. Sophie doesn't normally strike me as a small woman—but when she's caved in upon herself like that, she's suddenly very tiny and compact. I can barely see the wetness on her cheeks beneath the messy, mid-length black hair that's come loose over her arms. Concern instantly shoots through me, mixed with... anger. White hot anger. That surprises me so much that I stop short for a second.

I want to make someone pay for doing this to her. I'm not even sure it's a human being that's hurt her; the phone call could be about a relative in the hospital or some other spot of cosmic bad luck. But at that thought, I'm simply angry at the world on her behalf, as useless as that might be.

I force down the uncomfortable rage and clear my throat politely. "Miss Eddings?" I say.

"I... I'm sorry," she mumbles into her knees. "I left my things in the hall. I think I n-need to go get them."

That tiny stuttered syllable nearly does me in. I'm only a human man, and the sheer patheticness of her voice makes me want to gather her up into my arms and promise to fix things for her. But I'm reminding myself now that I've always enjoyed myself a little *too* much in classes with Sophie. I know I look forward to Wednesdays and Fridays, subconsciously keeping track of the next time I'll see her chewing on that old pencil of hers, staring at me with that sly half-smile, as though we share some entertaining secret just between the two of us. Every time she's shown up in my office, we've devolved into discussing everything *but* my class.

Sophie is a tough, brash, delectably *American* woman. She's whip-smart, hard-working, and quick-witted— always dressed in tattered jeans and comfortable shirts. She's hungry for knowledge, for problems to solve, for the opportunity to throw herself at new challenges. I've never thrown a barb her way she couldn't turn back on me in an instant. I know that she struggles with difficult things outside of the classroom, but she's still somehow leagues ahead of her classmates. If anyone could afford to cry in the hallway and miss a pre-exam review, I suppose, it's Sophia Eddings.

But of course, she shouldn't *need* to.

I sigh and kneel down in front of her. Mentally, I relinquish any hope of maintaining my professional distance. *No one could expect me to just walk away from a crying student*, I argue to myself.

But I'm keenly, painfully aware of every place we touch when I slide my arms around her and help her to her feet. The feel of her faded cotton shirt against my palms is a forbidden thrill. The heat of her body, the soft hitch of her breath as I lean her against me, the wideness of her chocolate brown eyes as she stares up at me, all make me want to close the gap between us and kiss her so thoroughly that she can't think straight enough to be upset about *anything*.

It wouldn't work that way, I remind myself forcibly. In all likelihood, I'd just be taking advantage of her shock and adding to her problems. *Get hold of yourself, you bloody twat.*

"Come on inside," I tell her, forcing myself back into the more normal rhythm between us. "Unless you'd *prefer* to cry in the hallway?"

At first, I'm worried I've gone too far—that I've badly assessed the situation and upset her even further, instead of making her feel normal. But Sophie looks away, gathering herself up with an awful amount of effort. "Who...

who's interrupting who, now?" she manages. Her voice trembles again, and another shot of irrational anger flickers through me. Sophie should *never* sound this way. It's a damned travesty, is what it is.

"How rude." I have to force the words out with a modicum of humor. "You left your things in the lecture hall. If anything, you're preventing me from closing up and going home on time." I know I'm pulling her closer, tucking her into my side more tightly as I drag her back into the lecture hall and safely out of view. "I hope you intend to apologize for the trouble."

The door closes. Sophie looks up at me with an awful expression that I can't quite decipher.

She bursts into hysterical tears, and now I truly have no idea what to do.

2

____

SOPHIE

I can *feel* the situation getting away from me. I'm sobbing into Professor Oliver's neatly-starched shirt in a half-darkened lecture hall, clinging to him like a life raft. He's stiff with surprise; his hands settle awkwardly on my shoulders. I want to apologize endlessly for putting him in this position—but I can't seem to find a convenient break in the sobs to do so.

Slowly, he closes his arms around me, settling himself onto the edge of a chair arm. He's warm, and comforting, and surprisingly strong. I feel *safe*. It's a shocking realization. For more than a year now, I've been scared, terrified —out of my mind. I've slept light, plagued by nightmares, worried that Jordan will find yet another way to burst back into my life and wreck what pathetic little sandcastles I've managed to build in his absence.

I suddenly understand how afraid I've been, and how badly it's drained me—because in this moment, just for now, that fear is gone.

My body takes all of this as a signal to give up the last

of my composure. I bury my face in his shoulder and promise myself to be properly mortified later. His fingers stroke my hair reassuringly. *I'm in heaven,* I think, even though I'm utterly miserable. I don't want this to end. As long as I'm in this deserted lecture hall, buried in his warmth, I don't have to face all those awful things waiting for me outside.

For just a second, I let myself fantasize. I imagine that I'm not a student. I'm graduated; I have a job; I'm steadily paying down my debts. I'm the sort of capable, put-together woman that attracts capable, put-together men like Elijah Oliver. I don't have to worry about an old boyfriend getting drunk and upset at me—no, when *I* get upset, there's a calm, loving boyfriend waiting for me at home, willing to hold me and soothe away my problems.

In my fantasy, that boyfriend looks an awful lot like Professor Oliver—*Elijah*, I think, with a guilty thrill. Maybe even *Eli.* That fantasy really works, for the moment, because he's holding me close, murmuring something vaguely comforting in my ear. My conscience digs at me, knowing that he'd probably be horrified by my thoughts. But I can't bring myself to shove them away. I've had a rough year; I deserve just a second of self-ishness.

Slowly—very slowly—I run out of tears. I lean my head onto his shoulder, too exhausted to move. I'm trem-bling uncontrollably. It's always a little too cold in these lecture halls, and my body doesn't have the strength to heat me up right now.

Professor Oliver shifts, leaning me down into the chair. I let out an instinctive whimper as he lets me go, and he winces as though I've hurt him. That human, worried expression on his face is almost more surreal than the fact that I'm shivering alone with him in the dark. "Just take a moment," he tells me, with a reassuring squeeze of my hand. "I'll find you something to warm up."

He steps away, and I feel very alone and very afraid again. I close my eyes and try to breathe. This shouldn't be so hard, I think—I'm just as afraid now as I was before he held me. But somehow, knowing that there's a safer place I could be makes this all so much more painful.

I force some steel into my spine anyway. I can't rely on someone else to hold me tonight—I've got things to do. I don't have a solution for my housing situation yet, but I *need* one anyway, which means I need to start planning. I swallow down my weakness and force away those tantalizing thoughts of throwing myself into Professor Oliver's arms and not letting go. He's got his own life to deal with, and I'm not going to make this any more awkward on him than it already is.

I need to move my things, I think to myself logically. *Which means I need a truck. Truck rentals are probably closed by now. I don't know anyone with a truck.*

A hint of panic rises up inside me again, but I ignore it ruthlessly.

I can leave some furniture behind. It's mostly ratty stuff anyway. I can take the important things, put them in my car. I'll find a motel for the night and deal with the rest tomorrow.

That's doable. That sounds good. It almost sounds like a plan.

A warm jacket closes around my shoulders. The intoxicating scent of cologne assaults me, interrupting my train of thought. I blink blearily and see Professor

Oliver leaning down toward me again, tucking his tailored tweed jacket around me. There's a strange intensity to the way he looks at me, as though I'm one of his research problems that needs solving.

I like that look. It makes me shiver in a very *different* way, even if it's not what I think it is.

"Oh," I rasp dimly. The word slips out before I can stop it. I'd been so determined to get back to solving my life without him that I'd nearly convinced my brain he wasn't in the room at all.

Professor Oliver arches his eyebrow at me again. "Oh?" he repeats. "How eloquent. I look forward to your short answer questions, Miss Eddings. With rhetorical skills like that, I expect they'll be sheer poetry."

I choke on a laugh. *This* feels normal. Finally, a thread of sanity. "I was planning on writing you a sonnet about binary search trees," I inform him. "But now that you've guessed my plan, I'll have to switch things up. How do you feel about limericks?"

"Compact and to the point," he says, with a hint of approval. He slides his arm through mine, helping me back to my feet, and I nearly lose my hard-won composure. He's so damned *warm*, and he smells so good that I just want to lose myself in him all over again. "I'll admit," he adds, "if you summarize binary search trees in a single verse, I'll be damned impressed."

I grin shakily at him. "There once was a tree from Nantucket," I start, "that kept all of its nodes in two buckets—"

He coughs in surprise, and now I *know* I have to keep going.

"—to search is O(h), 'till that tree comes of age; it's unbalanced and O(n), so fuck it."

There's an impressive silence after that, as he helps me toward the door. Finally, he says: "I refuse to believe you just made that up on the spot."

A hysterical, half-mad cackle escapes me. "I was the limerick queen of elementary school," I inform him triumphantly. "I can turn *anything* into a vaguely dirty rhyme."

Professor Oliver shakes his head disbelievingly. The rest of what I said seeps in then, and he presses his fingers to his forehead. "You just made a double-entendre about fucking a tree?" he mutters.

I glance quickly away from him at that. Something about hearing him say the word *fuck* so openly feels strange. It's not like it's not merited, given the stress I've just put him under—but it's another step over the professional line between us, and I'm still guiltily enjoying it.

He's got my bag over his shoulder, I notice belatedly. It's another tempting whisper in that fantasy of mine. *Someone to hold me. Someone who does things for me when I'm upset, just because they notice I need it.*

I'm almost disappointed to realize that Professor Oliver is a good, generous man, underneath that cutting tongue of his. I might have been able to take this crazy fantasy of mine a little farther, if it wasn't for that exact decency. He's shown me more of himself than he should —crossed lines that he probably shouldn't—out of a sense of generosity. The fantasy, I decide, has to stay safely inside my head. I'll indulge it there—for the sake of my sanity, for the sake of having *something* to be happy about right now. But at the end of the day, I know I'm going to help Professor Oliver put new distance between us as soon as it's reasonably possible.

"Thanks," I mumble shyly, as we head out into the parking lot. It's dark outside already—still a little chilly, since we're in the middle of December. A miserable drizzle of rain has started up, just to cap things off. It's not going to be fun loading up my car with a flashlight. But the longer I lean on Professor Oliver—*Elijah*, that fantasy sighs at me—the more I feel like I'm building up strength. I might just have the fortitude in me to get through this gauntlet and collapse into a motel bed at some ungodly hour. "I, um. I really appreciate this," I mumble. "I'm sure I'll be fine in a bit."

Elijah pulls a set of keys from the pocket in the jacket that still rests around my shoulders. He flicks a button and the sedan in front of us chirps, unlocking its doors.

I blink.

"I'm hardly going to let you drive in this state," he says, with a hint of acid in his tone. It sounds like the most reasonable thing in the world, the way he says it. "There's a halfway-decent cafe nearby. We'll get you a hot meal and some proper tea, and—" He pauses partway through, then sighs. "We'll get you a hot meal and some coffee, I suppose. There's no proper tea to be found in this hellscape."

I'm too dazed to bother protesting. I know I need to get started on moving my things—but the prospect of cozying up to my hot British professor in a cafe is too tempting to pass up. Instead, my mouth moves without me, and I say: "We threw all the proper tea in the harbor, just to spite you personally."

Elijah shakes his head at me. "Get in the passenger's

seat," he mutters. "And for god's sake, use your seatbelt, you colonial scum."

ELIJAH

What am I going to do with this woman?

I've been sitting across from her at the popular late-night cafe near campus for a good fifteen minutes now, ruminating on that question.

There's a bit of light back in Sophie's eyes, now that she's had a good cry and nibbled around the edges of a sandwich. There was a brief moment where she protested that seven dollar sandwich with that bizarre American stubbornness of hers—as though seven dollars and change is going to break me. I studiously ignored her, and added a coffee onto the tab as punishment. I've slowly learned that arguing with Sophie is the best way to make her dig in her heels even further. *Ignoring* her arguments just drives her enjoyably wild.

My lips twitch at the thought, before I can stop myself. Then, a *very* inappropriate image asserts itself in my mind, taking things a step further. I imagine how satisfying it would be to ignore her as she breathes my name, begging for mercy, as I kiss my way up her thighs—

"Thinking about fucking trees again?" Sophie asks me mildly.

I blink quickly, jerked back to the present. The joking remark hits far too close to home, and I find myself *flustered* for once. I'm deeply aware of the inappropriateness of the thought, but absolutely unable to banish it as I stare across the table at her smirk. The cafe is dimly lit, with plenty of private corners. It's a far cry from the sterile fluorescent atmosphere of a lecture hall.

"Fucking *binary search trees*," I correct her. "You have to be specific. There's an awful messy number of trees out there. Every time I think we're done coming up with them, someone else gets a bright idea of how to build their own special bubble sort/self-balancing/FUBAR-enabled binary tree implementation that will surely be different from all the others—"

That wicked grin of hers widens, and an oddly warm, gentle feeling joins the heat in my blood. It's good to see Sophie smile. It's good to *make* her smile, to know I've engineered the outcome myself.

"Are FUBAR-enabled binary trees going to be on the exam, professor?" Sophie asks me, with a blatantly bemused expression on her face.

"Yes," I tell her, with as stiff a tone as I can manage. "Right next to fucking binary search trees and short answer limerick questions."

She laughs delightedly, and the sound doesn't bother me. It's rich and genuine, and it feels like an earned exchange. We've built enough inside jokes between us in the last hour to last another full year.

I could spend another twelve hours just sitting here talking with her and not get tired of it. I normally hate social engagements without a particular goal in mind, but something about Sophie makes me feel sharp and alert—on top of my game. She picks things up so quickly; I *know* she could go far, if she can only work her way through whatever nasty business is holding her down right now.

Speaking of which, I think, *it's probably time to bring that up.* I've been avoiding the subject, hoping she'll get to it naturally on her own. But now that she's feeling stronger, I suspect Sophie has tucked away her misery and started figuring out how to handle things on her own. That independent streak is admirable much of the time—but there's such a thing as taking it too far.

I meet her chocolate brown eyes evenly. "Who was that phone call from, Sophie?" I ask her.

Sophie's lips part in surprise. The laughter fades from her face. I see a hint of fear there now, and I know that whatever has happened, it isn't done with her yet.

"It's... fine," Sophie tells me. There's a tired, lackluster sound to her voice now, and I despise it. "I was just caught off-guard, is all. I can handle it."

I narrow my eyes at her. "My shirt is stained with your eyeliner," I inform her curtly. "So either you owe me a new one, or else you owe me the truth."

Sophie smiles weakly. "I don't guess they sell those fancy Oxford shirts this side of the ocean?" she asks me.

"They do not," I lie pleasantly. The banter relaxes her just enough that she sighs and gives up, running her fingers back through her hair in frustration.

"I... I've been evicted," Sophie says finally. The shame in her voice is palpable, and I suddenly understand why she might have found the matter embarrassing to discuss. "There was an issue at my apartment last week, and my landlord doesn't want me there anymore. I thought I had more time to find a new place, but he..." She swallows hard. "He wants me out tonight. He said he'll change the locks tomorrow, and I think he'll really do it."

My anger surges back full-force, at that. "That cannot possibly be legal," I say. "Evictions take time."

Sophie shrugs tiredly. "There's no way I can afford a lawyer... so the technical law doesn't really matter, does it? I sure as hell can't find a lawyer this late in the day, anyway... which was probably part of the point."

She's right, of course. The keen observation cuts through my anger for just a moment. Even in her current state, with a hundred things commanding her attention, Sophie has picked up on that little detail. She's turned the problem over in her head, analyzed it from a number of angles, and started formulating a plan to deal with it.

"You know the university has lawyers for this sort of thing?" I say. "You pay student dues, so they're available to you."

Sophie knits her brow. "I didn't know that," she admits. "I just kind of assumed..." She trails off sheepishly. "I shouldn't have assumed. But I've never had a bureaucracy on my side before. I always thought of the student center as the place that takes my money and puts as much red tape as possible between me and graduation."

"Well," I admit. "It is *also* that. But it has its advantages nonetheless. I can put you in touch tomorrow—"

I cut myself off as a thought occurs to me. There's a growing hope on Sophie's face, and I wince as I realize I have to crush it. "Damn," I sigh. "They're already closed for the holidays. They won't be back until January. Maybe I can ask around the legal faculty instead. I'm sure one of them would be happy to draft a stern legal letter for you, given that it's an emergency."

Exhaustion sets in on Sophie's face again. There's a resigned practicality there that hurts to see. "I still have to get my things out tonight," she sighs. "It's not like anyone can stop that. And afterward... I don't know. What would I even be fighting for? The right to stay somewhere I'm not wanted? A monetary judgment that'll convince all the other landlords in town never to rent to me again? It's probably just best not to make waves."

I shake my head at her. "You are being *terribly* unAmerican right now," I inform her. "What happened to dumping all our tea in the harbor and raising merry hell? This British stiff upper-lip nonsense needs to end. Why, it's basically *plagiarism*."

Sophie shoots me a wry look. "I'm being *very* American right now," she tells me. "Assume all the rich people are out to screw you, and hold your tongue until you're rich enough to screw *them*."

"Ugh," I mutter. "How depressing. I preferred the ruination of perfectly good tea. And believe me, that *is* saying something."

This isn't much better than having Sophie cry in a lecture hall. I already know I can't just let her slink away on her own to desperately collect her things. I shake my head again and shove to my feet. "Well," I sigh. "You haven't much time, apparently. Ask them to wrap up your sandwich for the car."

Sophie looks utterly crushed at that. She was probably hoping to spend the next few minutes steeling herself against the evening. But I know the night's going to be long, and I'd rather spend the latter part of it finding her a decent place to sleep. "Oh, don't look so depressed," I tell her. "I'm going with you. I promise I won't abandon you until you have your things stowed and you've found a proper bed for the evening."

Her mouth drops open, and I have just a second to

appreciate the fact that I've stunned witty Sophie Eddings. "You *what?*" she stutters. "But you—you have class tomorrow morning, don't you?"

I roll my eyes at her. "I also have sick days, and the ability to email the class—from my phone, right this instant. I assure you, three quarters of them don't intend to show up for an exam review at eight-thirty in the morning anyway. I was under the impression you were nearly done with your degree, Sophie, you *cannot* be this dense."

Sophie's mouth works soundlessly a few more seconds, and I see that I've expertly disarmed any further protests she might have had by pricking at her temper. "Well, I wonder why no one wants to show up to your class, if you're always *such* a ray of sunshine!" she manages finally.

"Oh, it's quite simple," I assure her. "Deep down, human beings just enjoy being abused. How else do you explain the rent in this area?"

Sophie huffs, still reeling from the whiplash of our discussion. Instead of answering, she snatches up her sandwich and her coffee and stalks over toward the counter to get it packaged up for the road.

For myself, I'm not sure whether to be pleased or angry or wary of the whole situation. I'm pleased to have a benevolent reason to spend an entire evening with a woman I shouldn't be taking to coffee or holding in my arms or thinking about shagging against the wall. I'm angry that the world—and at least one particularly terrible person in it—is such that Sophie ended up needing my help at all. I'm wary of the fact that I'm still burning with the awareness of her presence, that my mind starts drifting toward excuses to be near her, to touch her, to kiss her senseless, whenever I lose an inch of my focus.

I can't let those excuses get the better of me. But I already know I want them to.

3

SOPHIE

I'm desperately glad to have a sandwich in my stomach and Elijah standing next to me as I survey the sidewalk just outside my apartment.

"You have *got* to be kidding me," I repeat. I've probably said it five times now, just because I still can't believe my eyes.

Elijah has no witty reply, this time. His jaw is tight, and he's crossed his arms. It's good to know I'm not just imagining the sheer injustice of the situation.

The entire contents of my apartment have been strewn across the curb outside. I can't even see it all properly in the darkness, but I know that what hasn't been picked through by curious passers-by is probably so wet from the rain that it's too late to salvage it.

Thank god my laptop is in my bag, in the back seat of Elijah's car. I try to focus on that bright spot, fixing it firmly in my mind. I can survive eating off of paper plates for a while. I can sleep on the floor if I have to. But all of my programming projects for the year are on my computer, and if I'd lost all of that work at the very last second, I really think I'd be looking for a corner somewhere to lay down and die.

"This is ridiculous," Elijah says coldly. There's a truly frigid snap to his voice that I realize I've never heard before. He closes his eyes and breathes in deeply. I can almost *hear* him counting to ten in his head, trying to calm himself down. When he opens his eyes again, there's a disciplined, directed fury in them. "Pick up anything you still want to take with you. I'm going to take pictures of this, for proof. And then, I'm going to make some phone calls."

It takes me a second to obey, even though he says it in that no-nonsense professor's voice he has sometimes. I can't get over how openly *furious* he looks. Even I'm not this angry on my own behalf. It's oddly affirming, having an independent observer here—confirming for me that I'm not crazy to feel upset over it all.

I force myself to look away from him, even though I could drink in that sight all night. Elijah, as I have mentioned, is a *gorgeous* man. And right now, he looks something like a knight in shining armor. Or... maybe not. He doesn't currently look like a man with chivalrous intentions. Part of me wishes my landlord was here, so I could watch Elijah tear him apart with one of his legendary verbal assaults. Another, greater part of me is glad my landlord *isn't* here—because I'm not entirely sure the conflict would stay verbal in nature. I'm not sure if I'd bet against Elijah in that matchup, given the muscles I felt beneath that Oxford shirt, but I certainly don't want to be responsible for my professor ending up with a bloody nose... or a murder charge.

I focus myself on sorting through the soggy pile of stuff that was once my life. My few paperback books are solidly ruined. Obviously, none of the food is salvageable. I find my phone charger still intact, though I figure it needs to spend some time drying out in rice before I'll feel safe using it. I find a stash of legal documents in a ziplock bag in my dresser, and breathe another sigh of relief. God only knows what someone could have done with my birth certificate and social security number.

I tuck the small stash into the passenger's seat and sit there in a vague daze. I feel like I ought to be looking through the rest of my things just on principle, but I already know there's nothing else to save. All of my earthly belongings are effectively in this car with me right now.

By the time Elijah returns from his phone calls, I'm laughing. I don't really *want* to be laughing, but I guess it's better than crying. The sheer absurdity of all this is not lost on me.

Elijah comes around to my side, frowning. He takes my hands in his and squeezes them gently. "That's all?" he asks quietly. "Could you not find anything else, or do you need help?"

I shake my head breathlessly. "That's all," I manage. "Jesus. I think I'm done. Like, not even just for the night—in general. This is so over-the-top, it's officially transitioned from tragedy to comedy."

Elijah regards me solemnly. "You need a bawdy limerick for this," he informs me. "Make sure it ends with the part where the head of our legal department sues your landlord until he cries."

I try to bury my face in my hands—but they're otherwise occupied with *his* hands. It ought to be awkward, but it's comforting instead. He doesn't flinch or try to pull away.

"I'll... compose one in the morning," I tell him. Every part of me suddenly feels raw and vulnerable. "I think... I need to get some sleep. I don't know if I can drive right now, but... if you don't mind taking me to a motel?" My voice comes out smaller than I'd like.

Elijah sighs and leans down to brush his lips across the top of my head. I feel his warm breath ghost across my cheek as he pulls back again. I have a weird moment of wondering whether it's a British thing. Maybe it's not as intimate a gesture over there, I don't know.

"I will sort you out a bed," he promises.

* * *

I'm not exactly firing on all cylinders. Maybe, then, I can be forgiven for wondering why Elijah needs a key card to get into this hotel lobby we're in.

"I don't know if I can afford a room here," I mumble. "Probably not necessary. I'm just gonna sleep, after all."

Elijah pinches at the bridge of his nose, as though I've given him a headache. "This is not a hotel," he says stiffly. "I live here." He swipes his card at the elevator, and my brain rushes to try and catch up with the implications.

"...uh," I manage.

Elijah raises that same damned eyebrow—but I notice he's not able to look me in the eyes as he does it. "Your eloquence truly knows no bounds tonight," he says. "Will you be gracing us with any of the other classic weasel words this evening? Perhaps a scattering of *er*'s and *ah*'s. A dash of *okay, right, you know.*"

It's an attempt to remind us both of our normal relationship. At three in the morning, alone in an elevator with my very hot, very sympathetic professor, I know I need the reminder. But it doesn't work this time.

I'm literally going *home* with him.

"This really isn't necessary," I mumble. I'm leaned back against the elevator bar, barely clinging to consciousness. I'm still wearing his jacket. It still smells like him. The fantasy world in my head is bleeding out into reality, and I don't want to make it stop... but I've *got* to. I'm quickly losing my filters, and I just *know* I'm going to say or do something we'll both regret any moment now.

"I think it *is* necessary," Elijah sighs. "You're not in a terribly good frame of mind at the moment. You've lost your home and your possessions, all at once. Whether you'll be fine all alone in a motel room or not is almost immaterial. *I* can't leave you alone in a motel room. I won't sleep terribly much worrying about you. So... here we are. You can have a proper bed. A shower too, if you have the energy. We can figure out a more permanent solution once we've both had a solid night's rest."

I'm going to sleep in a proper bed. *His* bed? My brain stutters to an absolute halt. Of course it's his bed. By definition, even if Elijah has a guest room, the bed in that room belongs to him. But if he doesn't have a guest room... if it's the bed he sleeps in himself... that sends a dangerous tingle down my spine. I'm warm just thinking about it, even as tired as I am. I don't even know how to feel about that.

All I do know is that there's absolutely no way we're going to be able to hammer our professional relationship back into the general shape it's supposed to be. We're both very smart people, I think, and very capable when we set our minds to something. But Elijah has held me while I cried and kissed me on the head, and now I'm going to sleep in his bed—and I'm pretty sure there's just no amount of gumption in the world that can undo that sort of thing.

ELIJAH

Most American professors—even famous, tenured ones —do not have the means to buy a condominium in Austin. In fact, the public sector here likes to champion long hours and impoverished wages as though they're a sort of mark of virtue. You should be so pleased to have the chance to contribute to higher education that you'll drive yourself even further into the ground for it than the fellow next to you.

Thank god, I say, for the private sector.

I'm not one to turn my nose up at duty to one's society. I teach because someone once taught *me*, and I owe it to the next set of programmers on down to teach *them*. But most of my greatest triumphs came before I accepted an offer to teach and research in Austin's thriving technological center. And those triumphs came with a proportional reward.

The condo isn't some garish penthouse, mind you— I'm still a firm believer in spending reasonably. But I suppose I do get a slight thrill out of Sophie's wide-eyed gaze as she walks through the door after me. The windows have a lovely view of the city; the counters are all pristine-looking marble, and the furniture has a tasteful, serious feel to it. And while the place as a whole is a little bit *cozy*, it's just enough space to leave me an office in which to shove all my spare side-projects.

The office is why I don't have a bed for her other than mine, of course. The place where one might normally put a guest bed is instead a full shelving unit full of extra computer parts. Across from *that* is a whiteboard with an embarrassingly long list of code ideas that I intend to finish writing someday. I doubt she'd be comfortable sleeping on top of a desk with three different monitors—only *two* of which currently work.

I show Sophie the bedroom and the bathroom—the only other rooms in the place—and search her out a towel. I should be ready to fall asleep on my feet... but when she closes the door and starts running the water, I'm suddenly *entirely* too awake.

Lord, I think, as I sit down heavily on my couch. *Sophie is naked in my shower right now.*

The image won't go away. I have her in my mind's eye now. It's *my* bathroom—every detail is clear and realistic. And there, in the middle of my tiled shower, is naked Sophie, with her black hair plastered to her breasts and her hands running soap all over her body. *My* soap, my mind adds helpfully. She'll probably smell like me soon. Or at least... some softer, more feminine version of me.

I *think* I'm wide awake, but I'm really running on fumes—and that's dangerous. It's been an oddly emotional night. And now, my brain can't tell the difference between degrees of trouble. I really shouldn't have brought Sophie home with me—no matter how miserable she looked, no matter how worried I was about leaving her alone at a motel at three in the morning. But if I'm already in deeply inappropriate territory, my brain wonders, what difference does it *really* make how much further I go? If she's sleeping in my bed, is it really that much worse if I sleep there with her?

(For the record, a more awake and less emotionally compromised me would have the answer to that question: It's worse. Definitely far worse. But right now, all of this makes sense to me.)

If Sophie wants you to do that, I remind myself forcefully. *Maybe she doesn't want you to touch her. Maybe she doesn't want you in that shower with her, washing her back, kissing her neck, sliding your hand between her legs...*

What was I thinking about again?

Lord, she's so upset. Some primal part of me just wants to drive that all away with mindless pleasure—but that could just as easily make things worse. Besides which, we're both tired and out of our minds. It could be taking advantage of her to even suggest such a thing. Sophie has nowhere else to go at this hour, no one else to drive her anywhere. She might feel trapped if I do something inappropriate she doesn't want, and I'm not sure I could live with that feeling.

The bathroom door opens, interrupting my thoughts. I look up, and my cock—already hard with the fantasy of Sophie, naked in my shower—jumps to rock-hard attention at the sight of the real thing.

She's standing in the doorway of the bathroom with that one towel wound around her, barely covering the necessities. Her face is flushed with the heat of the shower, her hair clinging to her naked skin. "I just realized, um, I don't have any... clothes..." Her voice turns breathy as the situation dawns on us both. Sophie meets my eyes, and I see her breathing stop. That flush on her skin deepens, and not just from the heat.

All of my carefully-constructed, rational reasons to stay away from her evaporate in a moment. Her eyes are fixed on me, and her breath has quickened, and I'm absolutely certain that she's thinking all the same things I am.

I'm up from the couch before my brain has a chance to catch up with me again, to remind me what an awful, horrible idea this is. I lean next to Sophie in the doorway, brushing my fingers along the naked skin of her neck. It's nothing I haven't already touched, already seen; that skin shows above the neckline of her shirt. But she shivers under my touch this time and nearly loses her grip on the towel entirely.

Sophie looks up at me with breathless anticipation in those brown eyes. And I know I'm not going to disappoint her.

She sucks in her breath. "Elijah," she whispers. It's so incredibly soft that I nearly miss it. As though she's testing out my name, trying it carefully on her tongue.

I curl my fingers behind her neck and bring my lips down to hers.

It's everything I thought it would be. It's glorious, heated, *necessary*. She gasps, throwing an arm around my neck to steady herself, and I slide my tongue inside her mouth to taste her. She still has a tinge of coffee to her— not unpleasant. The rest is all Sophie: sweet, fiery, and utterly unstoppable. Her other hand barely keeps the towel steady as she leans up against me, desperate for more. My fingers dig into her hair, and she whimpers approvingly. *How far is this?* I think dimly. *Is this further than we meant to go? Is this too far?*

But it doesn't matter. Because Sophie is kissing me back with a crazed urgency, running her fingers back through my hair in return. The fingers of her other hand are unbuttoning my shirt, which means that she's *not* holding the towel anymore. It's slipped away from her body, pooling on the floor beneath us. I can see her gorgeous, perky breasts in the lamplight, their tips rosy and erect with desire. I can see that dark nest of curls between her legs, already damp with need.

I can't stop myself. I slide my hand between us and dip one fingertip inside her. Sophie gasps into me, and I pause to look down into her eyes. There's a look of shocked pleasure there—as though she can't quite believe I've crossed that line. She closes her eyes and kisses me again, with a soft whimper of need. I slide my finger deeper, slower than she'd like. She's already so dripping wet, so slick and ready for my cock. It crosses my mind that she might have touched herself in the shower thinking about this.

She's got my shirt off now; her palms burn across my chest, eagerly exploring. But she's impatient, and I can't blame her; we're both wired and desperate. Sophie soon slips the button of my slacks and tugs them downward, freeing my very obvious erection. *That* gives her pause for a moment. Her eyes widen, and I'm forced to assume that not *everything* is bigger in America.

I kiss her again—harder, more demanding—guiding her hand onto my shaft, desperate to feel her touch. Sophie closes her fingers around me, moaning into my mouth. I stroke inside her in turn, and those moans become a higher-pitched mewl against me. She's getting close to coming. I drag my mouth back from hers so I can watch her face. I want to see that face, the first time I make her come.

She sees me looking down at her—and as she meets my eyes, I feel her muscles clench around my finger abruptly. She lets out a soft, shocked *oh*. Her walls flutter around my finger. I hold her eyes as she comes, and she flushes even more deeply.

I wait until Sophie's come back to herself, then slowly tug my finger away. There's a sexy, languid look in her eyes now that only hardens my cock more. It's a painful delay, searching my wallet from my discarded pants and pulling out the condom I keep at the back of it—but I slide it onto my cock and push her back against the wall, kissing her hard.

"Say my name again," I breathe into her mouth, as I press my tip against her opening.

Sophie smiles beautifully at that for some reason, and I feel a hard tug at my heart. *"Elijah,"* she murmurs against me shyly. The sound of my name on her tongue hits some tightly-wired nerve inside me. I shove inside her all at once, burying my face in her shoulder. We both cry out at once. It's an incredible, indescribable feeling. All night, I've felt helpless to fix anything, helpless to make Sophie feel any better. But being inside her makes me feel like I've finally grasped at something meaningful. The way she leans back her head in pleasure and sighs is nearly as gratifying as the way she tightens around me, drawing me in. I know for a fact she's not thinking about anything but me right now.

Sophie lifts her leg around me to let me in deeper. I

grab her other leg and haul her up against me with a hard, satisfying stroke that makes her cry out in surprised pleasure. She winds her arms around me fully now, trying to arch against me as I pound into her. It just drives me crazier. I need more of her, faster, harder, deeper—

Sophie tears her mouth away from mine for the space of a single moan. In the moment, close to my ear, she breathes: *Please fuck me, Elijah.*

I know she does it on purpose. There's a wicked little smile on her lips as she says it. I come inside her almost instantly, gasping as the thrill of that little phrase hits my nerves in an overwhelming shock.

And *god,* do I come. I've been wired-up all evening just from being near her—from trying to be professional, from dealing with the intensity of her emotions and mine. All of that tension releases at once in a shuddering burst of pleasure. "*Sophie,*" I moan in her ear, and she shivers in return at the sound of it.

Slowly, we both come back down to earth. The sheer desperation of our desire has been dulled, and it's far past time for those reasonable misgivings to reassert themselves. And for a moment, they do.

I've just fucked one of my students against the wall of my condo. And yes, I'm quite sure we both enjoyed it immensely—but that doesn't change the fact that it was definitely a poor decision.

Sophie sighs against me a second later, and a little of that worry bleeds away. There's a blissful smile on her face that makes me feel absurdly pleased, no matter how much trouble it's going to cause us both. "This is crazy," she mumbles. "Am I going to wake up from this, or is it really happening?"

I let out a long breath. "Ah," I manage. "Well." My brain still hasn't recovered its necessary supply of oxygen, I can tell.

Sophie chokes on a laugh. "Who's weasel-wording now?"

I haul her up into my arms, and she squeaks in surprise. It's a short distance to the bedroom, and thank god—I don't know if I could stay on my feet a moment longer.

I dispose of the condom and tug the covers up over us both, pulling her into my arms. "Tomorrow," I mumble at her. "We'll definitely sort this out tomorrow."

Sophie snuggles back against me with another one of those blissful sighs. "Tomorrow sounds good," she agrees.

4

SOPHIE

I wake up in a strange bed, with a pair of strong, warm arms wrapped around me from behind. I can't remember the last time I felt so good.

I've got the dim feeling that I should be upset about yesterday. I had a nervous breakdown, lost my home, lost my things, and—yes—it seems that I *definitely* slept with my professor.

The last part isn't a cause for concern. Actually, it's so fantastic I still can't quite believe it happened. One second, I was in his shower, vaguely touching myself while I indulged in those guilty fantasies. In fantasy world, Elijah had come into the bathroom and joined me.

In the real world, I stopped before coming, frustrated and guilty—and realized too late that I hadn't even bothered to grab some damp clothing from the stuff outside my apartment. I stepped outside, burning with embarrassment, to see if I could ask to borrow something...

And the moment he looked at me, I *knew*. I knew that he wanted me, that he was going to kiss me, that there was nothing in the world that was going to stop us both from indulging in that very delicious, very bad idea. And then, we *did*.

And now here I am, firmly planted in reality—with Elijah's arms around me and his very gorgeous, very naked body flush against mine.

I don't want to move on from this. *This*, here and now, is perfect. I'm warm, safe, and relaxed. As long as I'm in bed, I don't need to wonder about little things like where I'm going to get new clothes, where I'm going to live, whether the man behind me is going to wake up and gently explain that sleeping together is a mistake we have to rectify and avoid ever making again.

That thought sends the first real spike of anxiety into my stomach. Of all the terrible things I have to deal with, that strikes me as the worst. I've discovered that I really, deeply *adore* this man—in addition to which, he's *very* good at making me scream in pleasure. Only now, by comparison, do I realize that neither of those things was ever true about Jordan. Now that I've tasted just a hint of a relationship like this, how can I possibly tear my own heart out the very next day and agree to walk away from it?

Elijah brushes his lips across the back of my neck, and I realize I've tensed up in his arms. "Mm," he murmurs. "Well, that's a nice sight to wake up to." His fingers stroke lazily along the curve of my hip, beneath the blanket.

I flush and lean back into his touch. "Oh, look at that," my mouth goes on without me. "You *can* be pleasant when you want to be."

He laughs. It's a low, rich laugh that I've *definitely*

never heard from him before. I find myself caught between a fresh burst of attraction and a strange sense of surreality. Elijah would never laugh like that in a lecture hall.

It's damned *sexy*.

He kisses his way up to my ear. "I can be *very* pleasant when I want to be," he murmurs there. His fingers drift down between my legs, ghosting over my slit. I'm already damp, with images from last night running through my mind. He caresses me with his fingertip, stroking so lightly that I let out a needy moan. His other hand closes around my breast more firmly, offering some of the pressure I so desperately want. My nipple is hard against his palm, aching for friction. He's still kissing the back of my neck; sometimes, his teeth close on the skin there. I writhe back against him, deliriously pleased by the feeling of his hard cock pressing against my ass.

It's an entirely different experience from last night. I can feel him taking his time, savoring every touch, every sound that I make. Elijah clearly wants me again, and he doesn't mind letting me know it... but he's not in a hurry to jump ahead.

"Is there something you want, Sophie?" Elijah murmurs in my ear, as I squirm with need. He's still kneading at my breast, while the fingers of his other hand tease just along the edge of my slit. I try to press into his hand, but he keeps his distance, tracing me tantalizingly. "Tell me what you want," he breathes. "I want to hear you say it. I want to hear you *beg*."

My whole body shudders at the heat in his voice. I've never been in bed with a man so in-control. It's sexy and oddly comforting at the same time. I just want to let go and do as he says, *anything* he says. I trust that he knows where we're going, and how to make me come.

If Elijah talked to me like that in a classroom, I'd tell him to go fuck himself—more colorfully, more snidely. He'd shoot some retort back at me, and we'd end up bantering back and forth for a few exchanges. But here and now, I capitulate entirely. I want to please him. I want him to please *me*.

"Please, Elijah," I whimper. "I want... I want you inside me again. I want you to fuck me."

His lips curve up against the back of my neck. His fingertip dips inside me. Every nerve in my lower body seems to come alive at once, sparking with the pleasure of that touch, and I gasp. His teeth nibble at my earlobe. "What a naughty girl you are, Sophie," he breathes. Something about those words in that posh accent of his drives me wild. "You're so ready to skip to the end. I'm not done with you yet. But... your honesty *is* admirable. I suppose you deserve some kind of reward."

His finger slides deeper inside me, and I sob with pleasure. The pad of his thumb caresses my clit, rubbing there in slow, lazy circles. I can already feel the heat building inside me. I'm hyperaware of how off-limits this all is, and it makes every little touch feel that much more sharp and thrilling. He's already promised to fuck me again, in his own bed, and I know we'll get there. My fantasy is outside my head, and it's so much better than anything I ever could have imagined.

"*Please*," I beg again, because I feel the way it makes his cock jerk against my ass. "I want you on top of me. I want... I want you to hold me down and make me come."

Elijah sucks in his breath. I know that breathy sound

in my voice is affecting him. His finger slides in and out of me, faster, and I whimper in approval. "That sounds enjoyable," he manages. "I'll do all of that to you, Sophie. But first... you have to admit that you've been very bad." He sucks in a breath, and I can tell he's holding himself back. "Have you been a bad girl, Sophie?"

A second finger joins the first, and I moan loudly. "Ye-es!" I gasp. "I've been *so* bad. I touched myself while I was in the shower. I thought about my professor screwing me. I fucked him against a wall, and it was *really* good—"

Elijah tugs his fingers free and rolls me beneath him with a hiss of need. I barely have the time to register the dark heat in his gaze, and the way his tousled blond hair falls into his eyes, before he pulls my wrists above my head and enters me in one hard stroke.

I can't even breathe. I'm so full, so stretched out. I arch up into him wordlessly, trying to take him even deeper. He's looking me in the eyes as he holds me down, doing exactly as I begged, and I can barely believe the intensity there. I've given myself up completely, letting him take control of me—and it's the most delicious feeling in the world.

There's no condom between us this time, and I savor the feeling of his naked cock inside me. But even as he takes me again, he presses his lips against mine with a hard, frustrated groan. "I need to find some protection," he murmurs reluctantly.

I tighten around him, unwilling to give up the exquisite feeling of him hard inside of me. "*Please* don't," I beg. "I'm... I'm on birth control. I'm clean."

The revelation makes his cock twitch inside me, and he hisses in his breath again. He responds by pounding into me, swift and hard, making me cry out. His fingers dig into my wrists, and he's suddenly fucking me the way I desperately wanted, like he can't get enough of me. "God," he groans. "I'm going to come inside you, Sophie. I'm going to make you take my come, and it's going to be *so* good."

My body agrees wholeheartedly. I wrap my legs around him, trying to meet his thrusts. He drops one of his hands from my wrists to slide his fingers between my lips, forcing them into my mouth. I know what he's thinking about as he does it, so I suck on those fingers eagerly, holding his eyes as I moan around them. *Later,* I promise with my eyes. And I decide that I'm definitely going to suck his cock later, with his fingers tight in my hair and his hand forcing my head down into his lap—

He hits a spot inside me that sends stars blossoming across my vision. I give a muffled cry around his fingers, and he smiles wickedly. The next stroke hits that spot again, and *again*, and *again*, and I finally shatter apart beneath him, in the most intense orgasm I've ever had. I try to scream out his name—but I'm hampered by his fingers, by the weight of him still on top of me, holding me down. As my nerves run wild with white-hot pleasure, I convulse around him, and I feel him come after me with a strangled gasp.

"Fuck," he moans. "*Sophie.*" This time, I feel the hot load of come inside me. It's deeply satisfying, in a primal sort of way. I feel marked, *owned.* It makes me feel as though I belong in this bed now, where before I was only visiting.

Elijah loosens his grip on my wrists and pulls me into his arms, holding me close while we both shiver with the aftershocks. He's stroking my hair again, and oh my god, I *love* this man. The realization hits me like a thunderbolt, sudden and terrifying and perfect.

His mouth finds mine. He kisses me again—hard, at first, but slowly softening as the adrenaline falls away. I kiss him back gently, wonderingly. It's a surprisingly generous kiss—the sort of thing I'd normally expect early on in a relationship, long before a man ever held me down and fucked me. I feel like we've somehow done everything backward... but it doesn't much matter. That kiss is everything to me, and I don't care that it came out of order. Tears slip out before I can stop them, and Elijah blinks in alarm, pulling back.

"Sophie?" he says warily. "Are you all right? Did I hurt you?"

I blink a few times, shaking my head wordlessly. "I'm..." My throat is tight. "I'm emotional. My head's still doing weird things to me, after yesterday. I'm sorry."

His eyes soften. He pulls me in closer again, and settles my head beneath his chin. "It's all right," he murmurs. "You don't need to be sorry. You can have a good cry, if you like."

I don't *like* the idea of a good cry, exactly. But he's making me feel safe again, and cared for, and all of that just strikes right past my usual defenses. I shiver against him and cry again—quieter, this time, and for a lot of strange, mixed-together reasons. I'm so happy right now, and so worried, and feeling so not-myself. And while I was originally convinced that last night was going to be the best sex of my life, this morning has just proven me wrong and knocked last night straight down to second place.

Elijah holds onto me patiently, stroking at my hair and wiping at my tears. I want to thank him—but everything I might say just feels lame and not-enough, and maybe not quite appropriate. *Thank you so much for screwing my brains out and letting me cry all over you* would just sound bizarre if I spoke it out loud.

I calm down eventually—but he's still stroking my hair absently, holding me against him. I sigh heavily. *I love you.* The words are on the tip of my tongue, but I know they're utterly insane. I might be overly emotional right now... but even so, I know those are words you can't take back. As hard as it is, I have to hold onto them until I've got my head on a bit straighter, so I can be sure they're not just my hormones latching onto the first person to show me real concern in a long while.

Elijah is silent—but I can feel him thinking, now that we've both gotten more tension out of our system. Finally, in a very soft voice, he says: "I meant to discuss things this morning like a rational human being. I shouldn't have attacked you like that. I'm sorry, Sophie."

A shot of fear races through me. *This is it,* I think. He's about to tell me this was all a mistake—*two* mistakes. That I need to leave as soon as possible. "Please don't apologize," I beg. I hope the sudden desperation I'm feeling hasn't leaked into the words, but I suspect it has. "I... this is the only good thing that's happened to me in months."

My voice is thick, and Elijah glances down at me, concerned. His brow knits. "I've upset you," he observes. "I didn't mean to do that." He leans down to kiss me again, gently, on the lips. I'm still shivering with fear, waiting for the other shoe to drop. But Elijah pulls back and looks me in the eyes seriously. "I'm not kicking you out my door, Sophie," he says. "I enjoyed last night. *And* this morning. I'm enjoying... *this*, right now. I like holding you. Perhaps I shouldn't, but I do. The rest seems immaterial."

I blink slowly. The words gradually penetrate. But I'm not a hundred percent sure that he's saying what I *think* he's saying, and I'm too scared to assume.

"If anything," he sighs, "I'm worried for *you*. I can see how last night happened. We were both a bit out of our minds, so I'm not going to dwell on it too much. But your life is very up in the air right now, and you might realize later that you've made a mistake."

"A *mistake?*" The idea is so bewildering, I nearly laugh. How could this possibly be a mistake? Elijah is so astronomically out of my league, it's unreal. He's by far the most attractive man I've ever met. He's frighteningly smart, in-demand—at the top of his career. In comparison, I'm... a freshly-homeless, nearly-graduated college student, with a truckload of debt and no idea where I'm going to be this time tomorrow.

"I haven't made a mistake," I say slowly. I can see him watching me intently as I speak. "I think you're... fantastic." An understatement. My face still burns as I admit it. "I love talking to you. And I'm pretty sure I could spend the next whole week in bed with you."

That elicits a smirk from him, and I have to resist the urge to kiss him all over again. *God*, he's unbearably sexy.

"...but I don't want to get you in trouble," I admit. "And if I'm going to be honest, I *really* don't think I have much to offer at the moment. I'm likely to end up dragging you down in more ways than one."

The smirk disappears. I have the privilege of seeing Elijah raise *both* eyebrows at me now, incredulous. "You think you can drag me down, Sophie?" he scoffs. "My goodness, you have an inflated sense of your ability to incite disaster. I assure you, I'm not married to this particular job. I have headhunters reminding me several times per week that I could be making much more money just about anywhere else. And I'm *quite* certain I'm equal to the task of helping you straighten out your life." He pauses, frowning. "*Not* that I expect this sort of thing in return for my help. I want to make that perfectly clear."

I don't know what the hell I did to deserve this man. *I'm not going anywhere*, I think to myself, dazed. *You're going to have to pry me off you later if you want me to leave you alone, you crazy Brit.*

I let out a breath. "This is crazy," I mutter. "But god... I'm all for it."

Elijah eyes me skeptically, and I can tell he's turning the situation over in his mind the same way I do, searching it for potential flaws. "I'm thirty-two, you know," he says. "I have... ten years on you, then? Does that bother you?"

"Nine years," I correct him—though it hardly makes a difference either way. "I've had to draw out my degree a bit while I work. And look, there's no need to rub it in that you're older than me *and* somehow prettier at the same time."

Elijah coughs on a surprised laugh. He lifts his hand to curl one strand of my hair around his finger. "Don't fish for compliments, love," he murmurs. "It's unsightly. If you want me to tell you you're gorgeous, just ask me outright."

The word *love* sends my brain off into a spiral again. I

feel like I've blue-screened. He tells me I'm gorgeous, and my few remaining brain cells just scramble up in a mess. I'm staring at him, wide-eyed and dumbfounded, which only makes his smile widen.

Elijah tugs on my hair, dragging my mouth to his again. The kiss warms me up all the way down to my toes. "You are *gorgeous*," he repeats against me. He says it as though it's a taunt. It makes me want to laugh. "Absolutely stunning. You always look like you're about to go to war with someone. You have *beautiful* eyes, and I should know, as I got to look right at them as you came—"

I shiver and close my fingers around his arms. "You are *far* too good at compliments," I observe. "Do you know what that means?"

Elijah's lips quirk against mine. "No, I do not," he says slowly. "Please enlighten me."

"It means... that you are actually *quite* talented at being pleasant," I observe. "And for the majority of the time, you just decide to be an absolute pisser of a human being instead."

Elijah chuckles against me, instead of being offended. I figured that might be the case. He actually sounds *pleased*. "You're also so very *smart*, Sophie," he says slyly.

Slowly, it settles in that I'm not getting shoved out of this bed. There are a lot of kinks yet to work out, I'm sure —but I'm not getting dumped before I can even get dated, either.

Elijah kisses me again, and I think: *This is really happening.*

5

———

ELIJAH

I should probably feel more guilty than I do. I should have woken up, assessed everything in the cold light of day, and realized that I've been a complete cock-up in more ways than one. I took advantage of an upset student, shagged her senseless, and let her sleep in my bed with me.

But strangely, all the daylight showed me was a gorgeous woman nestled in my arms, right where she belonged.

I know I should have tried to discuss things with Sophie first. But while last night *should* have dulled the edge of my desire for her, it all came raging back as she nestled her round bottom up against my cock.

After that, it was a *very* good morning.

Now Sophie is out of excuses as to why she's bad for me—bad for *me*, hah!—and so far, she seems not only unbothered, but *enthusiastic* about the idea of continuing this mad thing we've started up.

We spend a bit longer enjoying the warmth of the

bed. Eventually, though, I drag her into the shower with me, and I take my time fulfilling all those naughty fantasies she had last night. I'm already thinking of all the things I have left to do to her in the next few weeks.

It's been a long while since I dated a woman—I was always wary of starting up a relationship in America, knowing that I might not stay forever—but I have a very focused, creative mind, and I'm already bending it to the task of how to keep Sophie pleasantly insensible. She's not utterly inexperienced, but I can tell that the partners she's had have been, shall we say, *ungenerous*. All I've had to do so far is pay attention to her signals, ask her what she wants, and actually give it to her. The fact that this shocks her so strongly is a bit depressing—but I have to admit that it's quite good for my ego. That said, I don't intend to rest on my laurels. I have plenty left to show her... and we're both going to thoroughly enjoy the process.

I'm still on this train of thought as Sophie slips out of my room wearing one of my shirts. She's left the top few buttons undone, exposing much more than a hint of her lovely breasts. The shirt barely reaches the top of her thighs—it does almost nothing to cover the swell of her bottom. It looks better on her than it ever did on me.

"I'm *really* going to need to find something to wear," she says apologetically. My brain has to catch up to the conversation, still fixated on that tempting cleavage. I blink and shake my head.

"Of course," I murmur. I briefly contemplate the idea that Sophie doesn't strictly *need* to wear anything other than my shirts if she never has to leave my condo, but the ridiculous fantasy passes. "I've already thrown your clothing from last night in the wash. As soon as it's done, I'll drive you out to find some necessities."

I see those stubborn calculations starting behind her eyes, and I know she's thinking through how much she can afford. I decide to head off that train of thought now. "I am paying," I inform her. "That's not up for discussion. I ran into some Jehovah's Witnesses the other day, and they told me my soul is in jeopardy. Clearly, I need to do a few good deeds for the holidays if I'm ever to avoid eternal damnation."

Sophie's mouth drops open at the sheer absurdity of the statement. It's exactly *because* of its absurdity that she's unable to formulate an argument against it.

But she recovers quickly, and I realize I've underestimated her yet again. "A few clothing donations aren't going to save *you* from going to hell," she tells me. "I'll buy my own clothes, thanks. You can go volunteer at an orphanage if you're so worried about your afterlife."

I turn and look her in the eyes, dead serious. "How much money do you have in your account right now, Sophie?" I ask.

She hesitates. It's not because she doesn't know the number. Every student in my class knows the number—because they're all dreadfully poor and trying not to buy one sandwich too many. It's a sad state of affairs, and I hate it.

"...I have enough for now," Sophie says reluctantly. There's a hint of uncertainty in her voice. "I have a shift at work tonight. I should get some tips from that."

Oh my *lord*. I close my eyes and slowly count to ten. Of *course* she's still working. Of *course* she's going to keep her shift, the very next day after losing everything she has.

I calm my irritation and open my eyes again. "You *can* call in sick tonight," I tell her slowly. I do my best not to imply that I'm forbidding her from work, or anything silly like that. But I'm not all right with any of this, and I need to let her know at least that she has options. "You have a lot to figure out today. I will *help* you figure something out, if you need to skip a shift."

Sophie frowns at me. "I *can't* call in sick, actually," she corrects me. "I don't have any sick days. And I definitely don't get personal emergencies off. My boss is pretty understanding—but if she lets me off the hook and corporate finds out, she could get in big trouble."

Sometimes—very rarely—I wonder if we ought to invade America and take it back for its own good.

Right now, however, I'll settle for slowly straightening out *this* particular American. "All right," I sigh. "It's kind of you to be concerned. I'll try and help you get sorted for work today. But I'm giving you my number. If you start feeling overwhelmed, *call* me. I will come and pick you up."

Sophie blushes. There's a strangeness in the air between us, and I know the lines between us are still shifting and resettling. How this is all going to work, I still have no idea. But I can feel my brain working on the problem in the background, and I know it's putting the pieces together slowly.

"...okay," she agrees quietly. "But I won't need to call; I just want your phone number." She flashes me a flirtatious smile that hits me right in the gut.

I have to dig her out an extra phone charger and plug

her phone in to put my number into it. I know I've already done far more forbidden things with Sophie than giving her my personal number, but it still feels like another rule broken. Ah, well. I can spend the evening returning all those annoying emails and phone calls I normally ignore while she's at work. I strongly suspect I'm going to make some poor recruiter's month tonight.

Just as I'm thinking on that, my phone rings, and I shoot it a bemused look. But it's not a recruiter—it's a different call I've been expecting.

I tell Sophie that I'll be just outside. I step into the common hallway, and close the door behind me as I answer it.

SOPHIE

Elijah steps out to take a phone call. I give him a curious look, but I decide not to pry. Things have been an odd mixture of distant and intimate between us today, and I don't know how much further I feel comfortable pushing things, even if I could.

He comes back in soon though, still speaking to someone on the other end of the line. "—I'm checking in with her right now, in fact," Elijah says. His tone is back to being brusquely professional. "You can ask her a few of those questions while I have her." Elijah shoots me a wry smile and flicks on the speakerphone. "I hope you're doing better today, Miss Eddings," he says. There's no hint of anything untoward in his voice, but his expression is teasing.

I've never blushed so much in such a short timeframe. I have to work hard not to cough. "I'm feeling... a lot better today, yes. Thank you." I glance at the phone. "Who am I talking to now, Professor Oliver?"

"Hello, Sophie," says a woman's voice on the other end of the phone. *"My name is Linda Blaine. I'm in charge of the university's legal department. I don't normally handle student issues, but Professor Oliver happened to have my number, and I owe him a number of favors now for straightening out my computer."* There's a wry twist to her voice that suggests she knows how very technologically inept she is, compared to the two people she's talking with. *"There's also the fact that your case is really quite appalling. I'd like to get the ball rolling on some paperwork as soon as possible."*

I blink slowly. Elijah's words last night had gone mostly over my head, but it's now occurring to me that he was serious when he said the university's legal department was going to sue my landlord. "I... thank you," I manage. "Really, I can't express how grateful I am. But I have to ask... isn't this going to make it hard for me to rent from now on?"

"It might," Linda admits to me. *"But I can help you with that part as well. So for now, I recommend that we take this one step at a time. As I'm sure Professor Oliver has expressed before, we are both very aghast at your situation and ready to get you through this. I'm told you have an incredible future ahead of you."*

I fiddle with the edge of the shirt I'm wearing, unable to look at Elijah. There's only one person Linda might have heard that from. I wonder if he really believes that. But now isn't the time to ask.

"Okay," I sigh. "I believe you. I really don't want to seem ungrateful. I'm just used to things like this backfiring on me."

"I understand. It's a big step to take. I'm glad you're brave enough to do it." Linda seems to sincerely mean that, but she doesn't dwell on it much longer. In the next moment, she's jumped straight to business. *"Can I ask if you were given a notice to vacate? It would have been delivered to you by a courier, taped to your door, or slipped through your mail slot. Anything like that?"*

I frown. "No," I say slowly. "I don't have any paperwork like that. My landlord just told me to leave. I thought he meant by the end of the month. I left him a voice message later, asking what I should do if I couldn't find a new place by then. He called back yesterday and clarified that I should be out by the end of the night."

"Do you have any emails, any voice messages on your side?" Linda asks. *"He only communicated with you verbally?"*

I sigh. "I've got a text message or two. They're a little..." I cast around, searching for a polite way to express what I'm thinking. I can't find anything, so I shrug and say: "They're in all caps, and kind of over-the-top. He's not actually a raving lunatic or anything. I just don't know if he knows how to type on his phone properly."

"Oh, that's more than fine," Linda assures me. *"I'm going to give you my official email address at the university. I'd like you to transcribe those text messages for me and send them my way. I'm sure Professor Oliver can pull them off your phone properly for later, but I'd just like to know what I'm working with for now."*

She pauses. *"If you weren't given a notice to vacate, your landlord is absolutely in the wrong. I expect we'll be suing him for breach of contract, for the value of your rent for the rest of the month, for emotional distress, and for plenty of damages to your actual belongings. In addition to the text messages, I'd like you to send a list of everything you lost and try to estimate how much it's all worth."*

I search around for a pen and paper—but Elijah hands both over to me before I can ask. I start writing down instructions as Linda continues asking questions and suggesting courses of action. It's a lot to take in, but it's also nice to have someone telling me exactly what needs to be done.

I'm thrown for a loop, though, when Linda asks me a question I wasn't expecting.

"Can you tell me what reason the landlord gave for your eviction?" she asks.

It's just another question to her—one more in a long list of bases she wants to cover. But I find myself frozen in place, reeling back from all the implications.

"Sophie?" Elijah asks me softly. His hand touches my shoulder, and I suck in my breath.

"My... ex-boyfriend," I say slowly. "I broke up with him some time ago, but he's been..." I wince as I realize the truth. "He's been stalking me," I say finally. It's a harsh term—but it feels right when I say it out loud. "He showed up at my apartment last week, drunk and upset. I didn't give him the address, he just found me. My neighbor called the police on him. When my landlord found out they'd been by, he dug until he found out everything... or at least, until he found enough. He told me he didn't want the police showing up at his property again. That's when he told me to leave."

Elijah's hand slowly tightens on my shoulder as I talk. I'm ashamed to realize I haven't told him any of this until now. I didn't feel comfortable bringing it up with him when he was just my professor, looking to buy me a coffee and help me out—but I *should* have brought it up this morning. Jordan is going to be a problem in my life for... god, maybe for *forever*. That awful thought makes my heart sink all the way to my feet. I can't imagine spending my whole life just waiting for him to show up again. If I get involved with Elijah, that means *he'll* have to deal with Jordan, too. That's the sort of thing someone should go into with their eyes wide open.

"Do you have a restraining order against your ex-boyfriend?" Linda asks me. She's not unsympathetic—but I can tell she's still in business mode, looking to help me in as straightforward a manner as she can. The atmosphere between me and Elijah is *very* different. I can feel there are things he wants to say, but can't right now. I try not to worry about that too much. I draw in my breath and steady myself.

"I don't have a restraining order," I admit. "I tried to get one. I left him because he was an alcoholic, and I was worried he might get violent with me. The police said that because he'd never actually hit me, I didn't have enough grounds for a formal restraining order."

That wasn't *all* they'd said, of course. The male officer I'd talked to had implied that I was overreacting—that somehow, listening to my instincts and leaving *before* my boyfriend had actually hurt me was the wrong thing to do. But the people in this room didn't need to know every awful, sordid detail involved.

"That's unfortunate," Linda sighs. *"If we could make the case that you're a victim of domestic violence, you'd have extra protections under the law as a tenant. But it's not the end of*

the world, by any means. Your landlord has definitely already violated the law, and you have a sympathetic case. I really don't think we're going to have much trouble getting a judgement against him."

I rub at my forehead. I'm starting to get a headache now. It's been a long few days, and this call has been far more stressful than I was expecting. But thankfully, there's not much more to be said.

"I think I have everything I need to get to work on this," Linda says. *"I know you have a lot on your plate, Sophie, but it would really help if you could get me that email as soon as possible. Ideally, I'd like to have my ducks in a row before the weekend hits."*

I nod sluggishly, before realizing that she can't see it. "Thank you," I say again. "Yeah—I'll do my best to get this all done before tomorrow."

"Excellent. Professor Oliver says he's found you resources for your living situation in the meantime. Is there anything else I can help you with? We have a lot of student resources that lots of people don't know about."

I raise my eyebrow at Elijah at the mention of my living situation—but he shakes his head, and I assume we'll talk about that later as well. "No," I say slowly. "I think I've got a plan, thanks. I really appreciate all of this."

"Of course. I hope things improve for you, Sophie. We'll do our best to see that they do." I hear papers shuffle on the other end of the phone. *"Well, I have a lot of work to do. I'll talk to you both later, I'm sure. Good luck."*

We say our goodbyes, and Elijah ends the call.

6
———

ELIJAH

I have to stand there in silence for a long moment, gathering my thoughts.

No wonder Sophie's life is in shambles. Judging from the statistics, she's lucky not to be in a bodybag. I have to push away that bleak thought before it consumes me. She was smart enough to leave before things devolved, I remind myself. She's being punished for that, in a way— but not as badly as she would have been punished if she'd stayed.

"I'm sorry," Sophie says suddenly. "I should have thought to mention that before."

I blink at her, confused. She looks like a kicked dog. Is she feeling *guilty?*

I shake my head at her, stunned. "Sorry?" I repeat incredulously. "Sorry for what, now? None of this is your fault, Sophie. I suppose I can understand how it might *feel* that way, given the way that people have been treating you, but it's absolutely not true."

Sophie picks at the hem of my shirt, still unable to

meet my eyes. "I... I appreciate that," she murmurs. "I really do. Everything seems a little clearer when I have you around. I know you're not exactly *unbiased*, but it's still good to have someone tell me I'm not crazy." She breathes in slowly. "But I still should have told you. This isn't the first time that Jordan has tracked me down. After the first time, my roommate got scared and moved out. If I... if I stay *involved* with you, I'm sure it's going to come up. It's an ugly situation, and you don't deserve to get tangled up in it."

I mentally revise my plans for the evening. This, I think, is not insurmountable. I'm glad I found out about it *now*. "I think it's safe to say that *you* don't deserve to be tangled up in it either, Sophie," I tell her. "I can assure you, I understand that you haven't spilled your life story to me in the space of a single day. You have bigger things to worry about." I tug her into my arms, and she sighs in relief. I only realize after I've done it that I didn't have to think about it consciously. I knew she was upset, and it seemed most reasonable just to hold her—so I did. That's nice, I think... but also dangerous. I can't do that in public just yet.

"Let's get your clothing sorted," I say finally. "I'll help you put together that email for Linda over food, after that." Sophie relaxes further at that, and I know I was right to suspect she'd need moral support for that part. "Tonight, you'll have work—*if* you still decide to go. I'll take you back to your car so you can drive there. Tomorrow, I *suspect* you'll be studying all day."

Sophie frowns at that. She has *my* exam tomorrow, after all. It's the last time I'll have to be professional with her. "Er... Prof-*Elijah*." She gets flustered on that correction, but forces herself to continue. "Linda said you'd gotten me resources on where to stay. Do you have an idea for where I can sleep tonight?"

I can't help but raise my eyebrows at her again. *Really?* "You're sleeping here," I tell her slowly. "Obviously."

Sophie's mouth drops open, and she gives an adorable little squeak. "But—but I can't sleep with you, and then walk into your class and take an *exam*—"

"Well," I say wickedly, "you don't *have* to sleep with me. You could take the couch if you really insist. But that strikes me as an unnecessary sacrifice, given that I've already come inside you *twice* now—"

Sophie buries her face in her hands, mortified by the frank discussion. I don't feel inclined to show her any mercy, given how rarely I'm able to strike her speechless.

"—and if you really feel you *must* forego my bedroom for the sake of your maidenly virtue, I suppose I can wait to tie you up and have my way with you until your exam is safely graded and you're officially finished with my class."

Her body tenses, and I know I've hit the mark. Sophie's under so much stress in her daily life that she's excited by the idea of not having to make hard choices in bed—of having *all* her choices taken away from her, in fact. The idea of being tied up already has her crossing and uncrossing her legs in anticipation.

"Ugh," Sophie mutters into her hands. She's fully aware that I've played her. "You're unbearable when you're smug."

"No," I correct her mildly. "I'm *irresistible* when I'm smug. I am smug most of the time, after all, and you're still somehow attracted to me."

I lean down to kiss her on the top of her head and leave to go retrieve her clothing from the dryer. When I come back, I can see a new anticipation in her eyes as she looks at me, no matter how she tries to hide it.

I smirk at her again, because I know it drives her wild. "*Would* you like me to tie you up and have my way with you tonight, Sophie?" I ask her archly.

Sophie snatches her clothing from me. Her face burns bright red. But to my surprise, she forces out a clipped answer: "Yes," she says. "I would like that."

I reach out to tug her back by the arm. Before she can react, I twist her wrist behind her, hauling her up against me for a punishing kiss. Sophie responds just as intensely as before, when I had her wrists above her head. The restriction on her movement makes her moan and arch against me eagerly.

I pull back just far enough to look her in the eyes. She's flushed and bothered, and I suspect she'd probably go right back to bed with me if I asked. But we both have things to do today.

"It's hard to keep my hands off you when you're so honest," I murmur. "If you're a *very* good girl, Sophie, I promise I'll tie you up tonight. I'll make you come for me all over again."

I let her go and watch as she regathers herself. Her face is flushed, and I know she'll be thinking about that promise all day long. Good. I want her to have something to look forward to after everything she's got to sort out.

Sophie heads for the bathroom to get dressed—but she pauses on her way there. "If anyone asks, er..." Her face flushes. "Should I just say I'm staying in a motel right now?"

I consider that for a moment. It's what I implied to Linda, certainly—though I never outright stated it. "I suppose so, for now," I say. I don't tell her that it won't be a problem for much longer. I don't want her worrying about the things on my to-do list as well as her own.

Sophie nods, and disappears into the bathroom.

SOPHIE

I'm staring at the clock on the wall at work, counting down the minutes until I can head back to Elijah's condo. I should be worried about a dozen other things, in spite of the progress I've made today—but somehow instead, they've all been shoved aside by the anticipation of that promise Elijah made to me. I've gone from being too tired and harried and wary to have sex to thinking about it every other moment of the day.

I force myself to go bus a few tables, to make the clock go faster. I work as a waitress at a mid-level chain restaurant in the area. It's far from the sort of job I hope to have once I finish my degree—but for now, it pays the bills so I can *get* that degree.

Speaking of paying bills—after much dancing around the issue, I reluctantly took up Elijah on his offer to pay for some clothing and basic necessities. He *said* he'd allow me to pay him back if I wanted, but I know he expects me to quietly let go of the issue. He's wrong, of course. I've got one more semester before my degree is complete. With that proper programming job, I'll be able to pay him back every cent, and maybe give him a bit extra as a thank you. I've kept all of the receipts and put them with my other legal documents so I don't lose them.

I *did* get through the email that Linda needed from me. I was dreading the idea of working on it all morning —but once Elijah sat down with me and I got some coffee in me, it was far easier than I'd feared. The hardest part were the details about Jordan that Linda wanted... but even that was bearable, with Elijah squeezing my hand every time I felt like hiding under the table.

What on earth I would have done without Elijah... I don't even want to contemplate it. I owe him more than just money, that's for certain. There's no way to measure how comforting it's felt, just having another person around to help me while I deal with all of this. After my last exam tomorrow—*his* exam, in fact—I'll be on holiday break. I ought to do something special for him as a thank you. I don't know exactly what, just yet, but I'll probably be able to think on it more when that last exam is over with.

My coworker comes by to tell me we're closing up, and I breathe a sigh of relief. I've gotten through another hard day. The rest of the night, at least, is mine.

And I know exactly how I intend to spend it.

7

———

SOPHIE

I call Elijah on my way back. At first, he's a bit distracted by something, but he soon shifts his attention my way. I ask about his evening, but he quickly diverts the conversation to the sort of subjects I probably shouldn't be discussing in public. I sit in my car for an extra moment, as he asks whether I'd prefer having my hands tied behind my back or in front of me. "*It very much depends,*" he drawls, in that deceptively high-class accent, "*from which direction you'd like me to fuck you.*"

"You know," I say finally, in a voice that isn't *quite* as steady as I'd like, "I'm starting to think you want me to drive off the road before I make it back to your place. You shouldn't contribute to distracted driving, Elijah."

He laughs. It's that rich, low laugh again—the one I never hear from him in public. "*I'm looking forward to seeing you,*" he says. It's not an innuendo; there's a sweet sincerity to the words that touches me. I can't remember the last time someone said those words to me and meant them. Actually, now that I'm thinking about it... I can't remember the last time someone said those words to me at all.

I park just outside of Elijah's building and head for the lobby. He's already waiting there patiently to let me inside—and from the very first moment I see him standing there, my heart does a flip-flop in my chest. I've always had a bit of a crush on him, but it's just so different knowing that he's waiting for *me*. He smiles and opens the door for me, and before I know what I'm doing, I've thrown my arms around his neck.

Elijah catches me with a bit of surprise. I sigh into his neck, surrounded again by the scent of his cologne. "I missed you," I mumble, before I can stop myself. It's the truth, I realize. I've been thinking about him all day, like some lovesick teenager. Now that I'm here with him again, everything seems just a little bit warmer and just a little bit brighter around the edges.

He closes his arms around me and pulls me inside. "I missed you too," he murmurs in my ear. The words don't seem to come naturally to him, but I can tell that he means them. The obvious effort makes me appreciate the comment even more.

Elijah slides his arm around my waist and heads to the elevator with me. Once inside, I lean against him, letting my cheek fall against his shoulder. He doesn't seem to mind; in fact, I can feel him relax a bit as I sink into him and absorb his heat. I've nearly forgotten his promise in the moment—I'm just so happy to be near him again.

I love him. The thought overwhelms me again, though I manage to keep it to myself. I figure there's little fighting it at this point. Whether it's just hormones or stress or some kind of actual, deep connection, it's a moot point. It's there, and I can't seem to stop it.

As soon as we're through the door to his condo, he closes it and leans me back against it, ducking his head to capture my lips. It's a slow, languid kiss—somewhere between *nice to see you* and *might I tempt you soon to do something naughty.* I melt in his hands like butter. It's so strange how I manage to out-stubborn him in every other circumstance *except* for when he touches me. I don't know how he does it—there must be some kind of black magic involved—but Elijah somehow knows just how to handle me in the bedroom so that I turn into a senseless, moaning mess.

Right now, he slides his tongue into my mouth, and I eagerly part my lips for him. He tastes like tea. I've learned that he prefers his Earl Grey with a dash of milk, and that he feels the need to make it himself, since *Americans always oversteep it.* There's a soft tanginess to the taste that I normally wouldn't enjoy—but I'm learning to crave it from instinct, now that I taste it every time he kisses me. I briefly wonder whether he has some sort of evil plan to addict me to tea—but the silly thought passes from my mind as his thumb brushes casually across my nipple. I suck in my breath and feel him smile against my lips.

Yes, I confirm to myself, Elijah is *definitely* playing me like a fiddle right now. But I suppose it feels less annoying because, in this *specific* case, it means he knows exactly how to make me feel good.

"Tell me," he murmurs against my mouth. "*Have* you been a good girl tonight, Sophie?"

The words instantly dampen my panties for some

reason. I'm brought back to that moment when Elijah twisted my wrist behind me and hauled me up against him. I shudder against him, now keenly aware of every little breath between us. His thumb circles my nipple through my shirt and my bra, and I need *more*.

I melt even further. Of course I do. It's *him*. "I've been *very* good, I think," I tell him softly.

His teeth nibble at my lower lip, and I sigh blissfully. Elijah tugs me back toward the bedroom, and my body buzzes with anticipation.

He's surprisingly gentle as he leans me back onto the bed. I was expecting this to be a little rough—but I enjoy the softness even more, as he grabs my wrists and pulls them together in front of me. He knots a black silk rope around them, and my pulse instantly jumps. It's tight enough that I'd have to work to free my hands enough to touch him, but not so tight that it hurts. In a way, it's just an implied promise—a suggestion that I'm not expected to use my hands to please him.

"Is that all right?" he murmurs, holding my eyes with his. "Not too tight?"

I nod slowly. "It's... it's good," I mumble shyly. I can't believe I'm doing this—not just letting a man tie me up, but letting my *professor* do it. But I am doing it. In fact, I'm deeply excited by the prospect.

Elijah tugs my tied wrists up to the headboard, looping another knot there, and I'm forced to settle back into the pillows. When he's done, he leans his body into mine and gives me a slow, considering kiss. I can feel that he's doing it to reassure me... but I don't need reassuring. I'm already hot with desire, ready for him to make me beg again.

"I'm not going to ask you what you want tonight," he breathes against my mouth. "I'm just going to take what *I* want."

Those words suffuse my whole body with instant warmth. It's a game, I know—he's tying me up because he knows I want it. I *know* he's going to spend the night doing things that I enjoy. But somehow, the pretense that I don't get a say is turning me on. I don't have to think tonight; I just get to enjoy myself. And I fully trust that Elijah is going to make this good for me.

His fingers trail down my neck, snagging on the buttons of the black button-down shirt I picked up today for work. Elijah pops a few of the top buttons open, exposing the upper swell of my breasts and the edge of my bra. There's a very open, appreciative look in his eyes as he takes in the sight. He snags his finger beneath one of my bra straps and pulls me toward him, and I suck in my breath. He's looking me in the eyes again, and it feels like I'm already stripped bare.

"In all seriousness," he murmurs, "do tell me if you need to stop. If you dislike something, or... no, I don't need a reason. Just promise me you'll say something if you're uncomfortable."

I blink, caught off-guard by the sentiment. It's the last thing I was expecting—but the obvious concern in his eyes makes me warm in a very different way. No one's ever shown so much tenderness toward me before.

I love you. The words are on my tongue again, desperate to escape. Instead, I shoot him a shaky smile. "I promise, I'll say something," I tell him.

"Excellent," he murmurs. "Though, I'll be honest—I intend to make it very hard for you to think about much of *anything*." The concern fades away, back into that devastating smirk of his, and he flicks open another button of my shirt. I can't help but notice that gorgeous blond hair falling in his eyes again. My fingers itch to brush it away—but my hands are firmly pinned to the headboard. I twist my hands a bit to relieve the instinct. The resistance reassures me for some reason.

"Already getting impatient, I see," Elijah observes, as he kisses down the column of my neck. His lips are light on my skin, barely ghosting over it. He parts my button-down fully, exposing the relatively plain black bra beneath it. I'd contemplated picking up something more exciting today—but with him paying, it would have taken on a particularly uncomfortable feeling. Still, he looks at me like I'm the sexiest woman alive, and I forget that I'm really wearing the most drab, work-appropriate attire I could find.

"You know," Elijah sighs, sweeping his eyes over my breasts, "I haven't spent nearly enough time enjoying *these*. I need to rectify that." He releases my bra strap, kissing the skin of my shoulder next to it—then descending slowly down the swell of my breast. His lips reach the line of my bra, and I feel his warm breath *just* above the place where I really want it. I squirm with need, and he flicks his tongue just beneath the fabric, grazing my hard nipple.

I gasp and rise off the bed just a little bit. Elijah presses his palm firmly against my stomach, shoving me back down into place. "Naughty girl," he drawls against my skin. "Stop trying to rush me. I'll take what I want, when I want it."

God, I'm already *dying*. I knew this was going to be

good, but I had no idea just *how* good. My brain is swimming with heat and desire. Every time he tells me what to do in that confident, authoritative tone, another stab of strange pleasure goes through me.

Elijah toys with the top my bra with one finger, sliding it down just far enough to expose my nipple to the air. He considers it admiringly for a moment, running his thumb over the tip. Then, he dips his head and closes his mouth around it. A loud moan slips from me, echoing in the bedroom. His palm continues pressing against my stomach, holding me down as he licks and sucks at that nipple, eliciting more sounds from me.

Elijah soon turns his attention to my other breast, leaving the first barely exposed. He slides a knee between my thighs as he does, parting my legs. I open up for him, though I'm still wearing my jeans, and he settles himself there firmly, pressing his weight down on top of me. I can feel his cock against me, already deliciously hard through the clothing that separates us. I try to rub against him, desperate for friction—but he simply pins me down harder with the weight of his body, holding me in place.

I'm going absolutely crazy in the very best way. "Oh god, please, yes," I'm whimpering, trying to urge him on. "Please, Elijah, *please*." I know he loves it when I beg— and sure enough, his cock grows harder against me as I do.

Elijah lifts his lips from my breasts to watch my face as I writhe beneath him, and I see his eyes darken with desire. He brings his mouth down on mine—hard, this time, and uncompromising. It's utterly different from that soft, gentle kiss before. He forces my mouth open, invading with his tongue, conquering me utterly. The more I make approving noises, the more punishing he becomes. He knits his fingers through my hair, wrenching my head to the side to grant him better access to my mouth. He bites down on my lower lip hard enough that I taste just a hint of copper.

He wrenches down the straps of my bra with his other hand, leaving them limp next to my shoulders. Then, he tugs the bra down roughly, fully exposing my breasts so he can massage them each in turn. His breathing is harsh, and I know he's enjoying this as much as I am—the idea just turns me on even more. My moans are getting higher and more desperate. My jeans are so damp between my thighs that I know he can't help but notice.

Elijah's fingers descend between my legs, rubbing along that damp spot, giving me just a hint of the friction that I so desperately need. "You're so fucking wet already," he groans into my mouth. "You really *are* delightfully naughty."

My head is spinning now. I can barely think straight, with his fingers running up and down the outside of my jeans. "Are you going to punish me, professor?" The words come out on instinct, before I can give them a second thought.

There's a pause between us. Elijah blinks in surprise, and I worry that I've crossed a line I shouldn't have, reminding us both of the professional relationship we're trying to leave behind.

But his mouth quirks into that sly smirk, and he snaps open the front button of my jeans, holding my eyes.

"I am going to punish you *very* hard, Miss Eddings," he promises me heatedly. He tugs my jeans and my panties down off my hips, pulling them from my legs and tossing them to the floor, and I whimper with newfound desire as the air hits my naked pussy.

Elijah brings his mouth down between my legs then, and presses his lips to the little swollen nub there. I cry out in shock, rising up off the bed again. He presses his palms to my inner thighs, forcing my legs open beneath him as he gently pulls my clit between his lips. He licks and sucks there, and I know I'm screaming now, bucking underneath his mouth.

He licks his way down my slit, dipping his tongue inside. "Oh god," I sob. "Oh fuck. Professor, *please!*" He swirls his tongue approvingly, shifting his fingers to circle my clit. Just a few more licks have me coming apart beneath him, crying out wordlessly as I orgasm. My head feels like it's floating a foot above me; I'm blinded with pleasure, helpless to do much more than ride it out.

He keeps licking me as I come. I can't do anything. I'm shuddering beneath his mouth, slowly surfacing back to rational thought as the waves of pleasure slow and finally subside.

Elijah looks up at me with the most arrogant smirk I've seen on him yet. It makes me want to shove him down and ride him until he comes—but I'm still quite firmly tied to the headboard. He slides back up my body and kisses me, and I taste myself on his tongue. He pulls back to unbutton his shirt as I watch, finally shrugging it to the floor.

"That," he tells me, "was not your punishment, Miss Eddings. It was not *nearly* enough."

I watch him heatedly as he tugs his slacks far enough down to reveal his cock. I fix my eyes on it hungrily, and he strokes one hand over it as I watch. He climbs back on top of me, pressing his palms against my inner thighs again to force my legs open beneath him. His eyes glint with anticipation as the tip of his cock presses against my swollen entrance.

"I'm going to fuck you harder than anyone has ever fucked you before," he informs me, in that crisp accent of his. "You are going to scream for me, Miss Eddings. And then, I am going to come inside you... and you are going to thank me."

The tip of his cock presses just slightly inside me, and I'm already dizzy with desire again. I want him inside me so badly, and I know it shows openly on my face.

His fingers dig into my thighs. His breathing quickens again. "In fact," he tells me harshly, "you're going to thank me right now, for making you come. Say it. Say *thank you for making me come, professor.*"

I can't take this. My blood is pounding, my face is warm, my head is dizzy. This is so fucking hot. I didn't know I could even *be* this turned on. "Thank you for making me come, professor," I whimper.

His cock jerks at the words. His breath catches in his throat. But he leans in closer. "I didn't hear you, Miss Eddings," he admonishes me. "Say it *louder.*"

Oh, *god*, I want him inside me. I'm squirming again, so desperate—but he has perfect control of my hips. "Thank you for making me come, professor!" I gasp out, louder this time.

Elijah kisses me hard. "You're welcome," he breathes into my mouth.

He slams himself inside me, and I'm already seeing stars.

He wasn't exaggerating before. He fucks me hard and deep, taking exactly what he wants from me. I scream obediently—not because I'm trying to follow instructions, but because I'm already close to coming again. I can't get enough of the feeling of his big, hard cock pounding into me, stretching me out. I hear him moaning too, obviously enjoying himself, and it pushes me higher. I love that sound, almost as much as I love the feel of him inside me. He slams into me one last time, letting out a ragged groan, and I feel him come *hard*, spilling his warm come inside me.

I come again with him, gasping out his name. It's the most intimate thing I've ever experienced. It comes with a tangled mess of wild, unexpected emotion. I want to cry again. I want to kiss every inch of his face. I want him to hold me—and he does, shuddering against me as his cock continues to twitch inside me.

Elijah kisses me breathlessly. Somehow, he finds the presence of mind to pry loose the knots that hold my wrists above my head. I immediately slide my arms around him and break away from that kiss to bury my face in his shoulder.

I have never in my life felt quite so full, so *perfect*. His fingers tangle in my hair. He kisses me gently over and over, tugging me free from my shirt and my bra so he can feel my bare skin against his. I sigh in blissful relief.

"You're so beautiful," Elijah murmurs. There's a distant wonder in his voice as he says it. He strokes the skin of my arms, my back. "My Sophie."

Those words make me shiver. *My Sophie.* I repeat them in my mind over and over, relishing the sound of them.

"Are you all right?" he asks me sleepily.

I grin, feeling dazed and satisfied. "No," I tell him. "I'm pretty sure you fucked my brains out. I need those for tomorrow—I have an exam."

Elijah laughs at that and kisses the top of my head. I snuggle into his arms, just enjoying the moment. I try to hold myself awake so I can savor it fully—it's the best I've ever felt, and I don't want it to end. But I'm so relaxed that I slip into unconsciousness, with my leg thrown over his hip and my face nuzzled into his neck.

8
———

SOPHIE

I wake up alone in bed. I can still feel the warm spot where Elijah was—I've cuddled into it, pulling his pillow into my arms. I blink slowly, collecting my mind. I can smell coffee wafting in from the kitchen-living room area outside the bedroom. It's what woke me up, in fact.

I don't want to leave that warm bed—but I'm eventually lured out by the promise of that coffee. I snatch up one of Elijah's shirts, pulling it over my head, and I slip out in search of caffeine.

There's a tiny coffee machine on the kitchen counter. I'm almost positive it wasn't there yesterday—Elijah prefers tea, after all. The coffee machine is just large enough to hold one or two cups worth; the pot is full, and the little red light shows that it's been warming on the burner for the last bit. There's a single empty mug next to the coffee machine, with a cheap red Christmas bow stuck to it, and I smile stupidly as I realize it's there for me. He must have picked up both things yesterday, while I was finding myself some clothing.

I fill up the mug and savor the first few sips of coffee, glancing around the condo. At first, I wonder if Elijah has left to go somewhere. But the office door is slightly cracked, and as I wander toward it, I see him inside, sitting at the desk. His hair is still messy from bed, but he's thrown on a loose Oxford and slacks already, and there's a steaming mug of tea next to him on the desk.

He's booted up a laptop and linked it up to the other monitors there. One of them shows an email client; another one has an IDE open. The laptop shows an SSH terminal—it's dumping some continual output to the screen. I'm not able to parse through it very quickly, since I'm not sure of the nature of the program he's running, but Elijah's bored expression suggests that it's going more-or-less as-expected so far.

I knock at the door, and Elijah glances over toward me. His lips curve upward as he sees me, and my heart flip-flops again. "I should just let you keep that shirt," he muses. "It looks fantastic on you."

I've still got that stupid grin on my face from finding the coffee. After that comment, I'm now smiling so hard it hurts my face just a little. "I think I'd better wear a *different* shirt to class today," I tease him.

Elijah raises a speculative eyebrow at that, as though entertaining the image in his head. "Now I'm half-tempted to see what would happen," he admits. "But no —you'll probably have to change."

I slip inside the office, glancing curiously at the screens again. "Is this one of your research projects?" I ask him.

"After a fashion," he says. Elijah leans back in the office chair and pats his lap. I laugh and take the proffered seat. He loops an arm around my waist to steady me, looking cat-like and contented. "I run the start-up lab," he explains. "So I mostly help those students with *their* projects. A lot of my work is just making sure that promising students end up in contact with companies that want them on their projects, and occasionally stepping in when they get stuck."

"Huh." I blink. "I'll admit, I'm surprised. I figured with your reputation, you'd be doing your own research."

Elijah grabs his mug and takes a sip. "Oh, don't get me wrong," he murmurs. "I have personal side-projects waiting for me to work on them. But at this point, most of my value to the university is in my business connections. I couldn't possibly work on every project people want me to work on, so I train students that can do the work instead. Every time someone tries to lure me away to their company, I'm able to suggest they put their money into the lab and get a group of students on it."

I have to work to get my head around the concept—but I nod slowly. "You're essentially training a bunch of baby AI interns," I say.

Elijah kisses the back of my neck, and I can feel the curve of his smile there. "It lets me dabble much more than if I were working on just one thing," he says. "And of course, I *do* enjoy ordering people around."

I shift in his lap at that, blushing. I set my mug down and turn to look at him. He's got one of those knowing smirks on his lips already.

I clear my throat. "Last night was... um..." I can feel myself turning beet red. "It was really good. *Really* good."

I press my lips together to try and hold in my embarrassment. "I think it was exactly what I needed. Thank you."

Elijah's smile turns oddly soft. It's another new expression on him that I wasn't expecting to see. "I thought that might be the case," he admits. "But there's no need to thank me. I quite enjoyed myself."

I lean in impulsively, brushing my lips across his. It's not a bedroom sort of kiss, or a hungry one. It's just... affectionate. I like the casual feeling of it.

He's still looking at me with that softer expression when I pull back. His fingers stroke absently at my back. "I think you should know," he tells me. "I was planning on asking you to join the lab next semester. I don't normally bother asking bachelors students, but I thought you'd do well there."

I'm told you have an incredible future ahead of you. That's what Linda said to me on the phone call. Now I'm sure it was Elijah that told her that. I'm so touched by the revelation that my smile wavers, turning just a little bit watery. "Oh," I manage softly.

"Obviously, that seems like a conflict of interest now," Elijah sighs. "But I did want you to know. You're one of the smartest, most hardworking students I've come across yet. Even if you don't end up in AI, I'm sure you'll excel at whatever you *do* choose. I'm not the only one who thinks so—Professor Winslow adores you. She said if I don't snatch you up, she might try to lure you into the computer side of law enforcement."

Professor Winslow? I frown as I remember the severe, steel-haired professor in question. I finished my final in her *Computer Crimes* class only three days ago. I find it hard to imagine that old ex-cop *adoring* anyone—but if

Elijah thinks it's worth mentioning, then I suppose Professor Winslow must have said something at least vaguely resembling those words.

I lean my head against his shoulder. It's hard to look at him while he's complimenting me like this. I'm so used to him throwing barbs my way that it's a bit shocking to hear the opposite.

Still, a hint of habitual insecurity weasels its way into my mind. I don't *feel* like a smart student. I work hard, of course, but I've often looked around at my fellow students and felt like I fall short. They all have such fantastic side-projects—building little robots from scratch, contributing to open source distributions. I've never had the time or the money to pursue that sort of hyper-focused passion. And if I'm utterly honest with myself... I'm not sure that I *want* to. I didn't go into computer science because it was something I loved. Compared to the students who *do* genuinely love it, I feel like a fraud.

"I appreciate that," I tell him. "I really do. But... I'm not passionate about my degree." It's a quiet, shameful admission. "I chose it because I thought it would get me a secure, decently-paying job. I just... I was so lucky to get my scholarship. I didn't want to waste the opportunity and end up without any options. But I don't know if I'm ever going to be any kind of real expert."

Elijah is silent for a moment. His thumb keeps rubbing across my back, and I wonder what he's thinking. Finally, he says: "I don't think passion has anything to do with it, Sophie. You don't have to be utterly obsessed with something in order to be good at it."

He shifts me so that he can look me in the eyes, and I

see a thoughtful look there. "People tell me I'm at the top of my field," he says. "I still think that's rubbish. Most days, I feel like I've somehow fooled everyone—that anyone could do what I'm doing, if they read enough textbooks and white-papers, and wrote enough code."

I can feel my eyebrows rising as he speaks. I can't believe what I'm hearing. *Holy hell.* Elijah Oliver isn't exactly a movie star—but within certain small technological circles, he might as well be one. If even *he* feels like a fraud, I find myself wondering if *anyone* in our industry believes they're worth anything.

Elijah takes a long breath and fixes me with a hard look. "But not everyone *is* doing what I'm doing," he says. "And that's the point. And at the end of the day, the reason I'm in demand isn't because I'm a genius—it's for a very different reason. Can you guess what it is?"

I frown. I can hear in his tone that he expects me to actually try and answer the question. He wants to know whether I can puzzle out his line of thought. I knit my brow and chew on what I know of him personally.

A potential answer comes to me. I'm not certain of it —but I turn it over a few times and decide that it's still an *interesting* answer, even if it's not the right one.

"Your contacts," I say finally. "You know a lot of people by now. And... I think people actually like you, on the whole. Even though you're a bastard to most of them."

Elijah's lips twitch at that. "I'm afraid that's one of my advantages you can't emulate," he tells me. "Americans will endure just about anything if you say it in a British accent." He tickles lightly at my side, as though to demonstrate, and he smiles as I squirm. "More realistically—I'm good at trading favors. I know my limits, and when I hit an area I'm not equipped to handle, I go and ask for help with it. And when I see an opportunity to do favors for *other* people, I do them."

I blink as a few things click into place all at once. I remember something else that Linda said: *Professor Oliver happened to have my number, and I owe him a number of favors now for straightening out my computer.*

"You gave IT support to Linda," I say.

Elijah shoots me a lopsided smile. "Ah, you caught that," he says. "You're right, yes. I had a meeting with her when I first came on at the university, to go over the standard boilerplate agreements. I noticed she was having trouble with her computer monitor, and I made a few suggestions. She was so immediately grateful that I told her she could call me in the future if she needed anything."

"That's kind of crazy," I laugh. "There's a whole department at the university she could call for that. It's probably not even within your expertise."

Elijah raises an eyebrow at me. "It's not as mad as you might think," he says. "Linda is a very accomplished woman within her field. It embarrasses her to admit that she doesn't know things, even when they're not *supposed* to be within her expertise. It makes her feel better to call someone she knows personally when she has questions. That way, there's no ticket in the system, and no IT interns gossiping about how stupid she is over their lunch breaks."

I bite at my lip, thinking that over. It's an unexpectedly empathetic answer. I'm honestly surprised that it came from the man in front of me. "That's very kind of you," I tell him. Some of my skepticism must come out in my voice, because he grins.

"It's both kind and selfish, all at once," Elijah replies neatly. "I don't *just* do favors for important people—you never know who might *become* important later. But I can't say that the networking aspect of it doesn't figure in. Anyway, this is all to say... you ought to remember that even if you don't *feel* special, you still have your own sort of superpower, as a technologically literate woman. People like Linda trust that you hang the moon when it comes to anything computer-related. If you take pains to solve those little problems for people, you'll also find it a nice balm for your confidence."

I slide my arms around his neck, shifting for a more comfortable position. I'm still thinking about what he's said. It niggles at me for some reason, and I'm not sure why.

"...I don't like asking people for favors," I admit finally. "It just rubs me the wrong way for some reason."

"Oh, *believe* me," Elijah says dryly. "I've noticed." There's a hint of a long-suffering air to the words. "You are so terribly determined to be self-sufficient, Sophie. Sometimes I wonder if you'd ask someone for a bottle of water if you were literally on fire."

I roll my eyes. "It's not fair to ask other people to handle my shit," I tell him.

Elijah tucks his arms around me. I feel safe again. I don't like to admit to myself that he is, in fact, *handling my shit*. But it all seems so reasonable from his perspective, when he lays it out for me. I *also* hate that. It makes me feel like I've spent my life so far being obstinate for no reason, instead of being considerate of others, like I'd believed.

"Why haven't you called up your parents for help, Sophie?" Elijah asks me suddenly. From the sound of his voice, I can tell he knows he's hit on something important.

I close my eyes. This is another subject I don't particularly want to face. But it's relevant to my situation. "I had a very bad fight with my father." I say it evenly, though the reality of the situation is far, far worse. A *fight* with family is normally where you disagree and get snappy with one another. This one involved far more screaming and throwing of breakable objects.

I take a breath. "He's a very... conservative man. That's a mild way to put it. I guess he's what you'd call a fundamentalist. When I got my scholarship, I knew it was my chance to get out of the house and never come back. I told him as much. Maybe I shouldn't have—but I spent *years* holding my tongue, letting him tell me what to do. It was just so freeing to be able to tell him to fuck off and leave me alone forever."

Elijah leans us both back in the chair. I can feel that quick-witted mind of his ticking through things, formulating connections... but I'm not sure I know exactly where it's headed.

"Do you know what I think?" Elijah says finally. "I think you're *predisposed* to avoid asking for help. If it's always come with such controlling strings attached, it makes sense that you'd avoid tangling yourself up with someone else who might use it to control you."

I blink. That's... a very reasonable hypothesis, actually.

"I guess that's possible," I admit. "I'll have to think more about that."

"Hm," Elijah murmurs. "Think more about it while you finish your coffee. And... preferably, while you study." He slaps me across the ass, and I yelp in indignation, scrambling off his lap. "You won't be getting an A just because you're sleeping with the teacher," he adds with a smirk. "I *might* consider extra credit if you write me another limerick, however. I admit, I found that entertaining."

I shoot him a dirty look. "I think it's fair to remind you that *you* kissed me," I tell him. "It's not like I walked into your office and offered you a blow job."

Elijah's eyes unfocus for a second, and I know he's now imagining that scenario with relish. "You should absolutely do that, Sophie," he sighs. "*After* I've turned in your final grades, of course."

I roll my eyes at him and grab my coffee. "You're impossible to shame," I mutter. Much as I wish I could, I can't quite keep the admiration from my voice, though. I'm beginning to wish I was a little more like him and a little less like me, when it comes to shame.

I do go pull out my laptop and bring up my notes, however. It's not like I was slacking off in class before—but I'm especially determined to ace my exam *now*. I can't imagine the awful embarrassment I'd feel if I failed, after all those compliments to my intelligence.

When I get dressed and grab my keys to leave for the university, I leave a little limerick about bubble sorts scribbled on the edge of one of his notepads.

9

ELIJAH

I'm still thinking about that conversation with Sophie, even after I've run through my emails and answered a few student questions. Every time I think I'm done working out implications, I find another interesting connection.

Sophie is exactly the sort of woman who normally falls prey to abuse. She's already isolated from her family, with very few resources to her name. The more I think about it, the more shocked I am that Sophie convinced herself to leave such an awful relationship when she did. I suppose it helps that she'd just had practice cutting ties with one overbearing man and figuring things out on her own.

The very last thing I want to do is continue that pattern with her. The idea that I might be taking advantage of Sophie's vulnerable state bothers me. I do want to help her—in fact, I'm more interested in helping her than I am in teaching. I'm more interested in Sophie's situation than I am in this start-up lab, or even in the side-projects that have been carefully waiting for my attention again, once I'm done with this teaching job.

But every time I do something even halfway considerate for her, she looks at me as though I'm some sort of superhero. As lovely as that is for my ego, it's just not right. Most of what I've done for Sophie ought to be simple baseline humanity. I want to believe I would have picked her up off the floor and helped her with her living situation either way, even if I wasn't already attracted to her. Granted, I certainly wouldn't have tied her up and had my way with her—but I might have found her some other, less explicit way to unwind her stress.

It bothers me that Sophie might end up attached to me just because I'm not utterly awful to her. She could probably find not-awful in some man her own age, who's never been in a position of power over her at all.

"Oh, listen to yourself," I mutter, as I shut down my laptop and start packing up my things. I've just finished convincing Sophie that she's got worth, even if she can't immediately see it. I've never had trouble going after what I want before, even if I wasn't strictly certain I deserved it. I *know* I want this woman in my life. And I know I intend to treat her well. Sophie won't ever need to wonder what she's missing out on; I'll make sure she's got plenty of affection, and witty conversation, and mind-blowing sex to keep her content.

I blink as I pass the coffee table in the living room. The pad of paper I gave Sophie to write down Linda's instructions is out; there's something scribbled in large, curly script on the front page.

"Discrete items all in a bundle.

You might say they're each in their bubble.

We go through and swap,
Put the lower on top;
But don't use this on any real puzzle."

I stare at the limerick for a good long while. There's a little bubble sort implementation beneath it, with each pass clearly shown in-order. At the very bottom is a little hand-drawn heart, as though I've just read a love letter.

A sudden, bewildering thought occurs to me as I read the silly poem again.

"I'm fairly sure I love this woman," I declare to the empty room.

I tear off the poem and fold it up, shoving it into my pocket. It leaves a broad smile on my face, all the way to the university.

SOPHIE

I imagine I can feel the other students staring at me as I sit down in the lecture hall and wait. They're not *actually* staring at me—I know that. But my brain is wired, and I feel like a guilty criminal hiding a secret. Which is... stupid. I know Elijah isn't the sort to go easy on me. If anything, he'll probably grade me harder, just to compensate for any bias he has.

"Hey," says my classmate Gina, from my other side. I jump and look over at her with wide eyes, and she snorts at my reaction. "I had to miss the review," she tells me. "Work called me in at the last minute. Did Professor Oliver go over binary search trees?"

I nearly choke on my laughter. "Oh," I wheeze. "Uh. In a way. Boy, have I got a mnemonic for you." I write out my first limerick for her, and we both devolve into childish snickers for a bit.

Elijah heads into class a few minutes later, and I find myself in the utterly surreal position of seeing him at the front of class again. Before, I realize, my brain always put a subtle mental separation between us. As much as we interacted—as much as I sometimes fantasized about him—I still did my best not to think of him as a normal human being with a whole life of his own. Now that I know him better, I don't have that separation. I don't respect him just because he's standing at the front of class. I respect him because he's smart, and funny, and oddly generous to the people around him.

Elijah's eyes sweep over me, and he smiles. It's that softer, more genuine smile—the one he never uses here in class. I look down at my bag, blushing furiously. I could look at that smile all day.

Next to me, Gina heaves a tiny sigh. "Oh, I'm gonna miss *him* next semester," she mumbles to me, as the tests start filtering up toward us. "I think I've got three old balding guys running my next classes. Not a single nice accent among them. Hey—do you think if I bombed the test, I could retake this class?"

A surge of confused, uncomfortable jealousy runs through me, even though I know she's joking. I have to swallow down my irrational reaction before I respond. "That depends," I say. "Do you want to sell your first-born child for an extra class worth of tuition?"

Gina shakes her head mournfully. "Sometimes I wish I could," she says. "But I'm told people frown on slavery these days, even if your kid *does* draw all over the walls with magic marker."

"You can discuss your black market dealings *after* the exam is over, ladies," Elijah says from the aisle next to us. I look up and see him standing next to our row. He smiles again. "Best of luck," he says. He winks and heads back down toward the desk below.

Oh, *lord.* I'm sure that was meant for me—but now I'm *definitely* distracted.

"Sweet baby Jesus," Gina says faintly next to me. "I think I can die a happy woman now. Did he just *wink* at me?"

"Oh, yes," I mumble, staring down at the exam that's just filtered up toward me. "Definitely at you."

My brain is now *swimming* with images of Elijah kissing my breasts, working his way down between my legs. I remember the way he breathed my name as he fucked me. I remember the command he gave me last night.

"Say thank you for making me come, professor."

I am suddenly *very* uncomfortable at my desk. I have to cross my legs and take a few steadying breaths.

I open the first page and let out a sigh of relief as I see the questions there. I *am* well-prepared for this exam. That's good—because I can't imagine what I'd do if I had to concentrate right now.

I shove away all of those admittedly-very-pleasant thoughts, and do my best to get to work.

I'm not the first to finish the exam—I think that's fair, given my unexpected handicap. But I'm still *one* of the first. I give my answers another careful once-over, wondering if I ran through it too fast and missed something. But everything feels very straightforward, and I can't find any errors. Finally, I push to my feet and walk down the aisle to drop my completed exam on Elijah's desk.

He looks up at me, and this time he smirks in that way I'm more used to seeing. "Already done, Miss Eddings?" he asks.

"Quite done," I tell him.

Elijah leans back in his chair. "Well. It's been an honor to teach you." His green eyes flicker with mirth. "This is where you say *thank you, professor,*" he teases.

My whole body heats up at the words. My mouth drops open just a little bit. I can see in his expression that he knows *exactly* what he's just done to me.

I narrow my eyes, and lean over the desk toward him.

"*Thank you, professor,*" I whisper breathily, just quiet enough for him to hear. I use the exact same tone from the bedroom, utterly shameless in my intonation.

The smirk fades slowly from Elijah's face—and I know I've just evened the score. He'll be thinking about that breathy tone for the rest of this interminable exam... while I'm perfectly free to leave and do what I want with the rest of the evening.

And I do. I flounce away victoriously, with a vengeful little smile on my lips.

* * *

I type an innocent text message to Elijah not long after I leave the classroom.

SOPHIE: Dinner later?

My phone dings softly with a response, only a few seconds later.

ELIJAH: That was cruel. And yes. I'll meet you at the cafe.

I grin at the screen. Already, I feel more free. My semester is over. My legal case is being handled. The boyfriend of my dreams will be sitting down to dinner with me soon. I'm hopeful that winter break will give me just enough breathing room to go find another apartment and get things back on track. All I have to do is last one more semester, and then I can search out a halfway-decent job in the tech sector with my shiny new degree.

For years, I've convinced myself to get up each morning and keep going by promising myself that things will get better. But this is the first time I really, truly feel like it might be the truth.

I head out into the parking lot, searching out my car in the darkness. I hit the button on my keychain, and a light blinks to my right, reminding me that I parked near the far end.

Someone grabs my arm from behind. I shriek in surprise and try to pull free, but they've got me in a vice-like grip.

I know the hand on my arm.

"Sophie."

The simple sound of my name brings everything crashing straight down.

Jordan is standing behind me, still holding tightly onto my arm. He's just as tall as I remember—but also somehow smaller, as I subconsciously compare him to Elijah and realize he's a few inches shorter. Jordan's dark hair is clean-cut, and he's wearing a nice long-sleeve shirt and jeans—but his eyes are bloodshot and unfocused, and I know he's either been drinking or else he's freshly hung-over.

Fear jumps into my throat. I'm in a dark parking lot. This is the latest class period in the day, and I've finished my exam far too early. The chances that anyone is likely to come outside in the next few minutes are slim to none.

"I want to talk," Jordan tells me. There's a slight slur to his words—but not so that most people would notice. He's always had that golden-boy look to him that convinces people he's harmless and charming. *Just one of the boys.*

"I don't want to talk right now," I tell him, as calmly as I can manage. The last thing I want is to set him off by being too harsh... but I can't afford to give him an inch, either. "I don't even know how you knew I'd be here."

Jordan doesn't answer to that. He never does. I know he weasels information out of my friends, my classmates, my professors—but I never know which ones. "We're hitting the bar tonight, Sophie," he tells me. "I want you to come. I'll buy you a drink. You're done with exams, right?"

I suck in my breath. He's started off with the reasonable tone. It always *starts* there. The more I refuse him, though, the less reasonable things will become. "I have work," I lie. "I can't just go off with you, even if I wanted to."

Jordan frowns darkly, and I know I've already made some kind of mistake. "Your restaurant closes in like an hour," he says. He jerks me back by the arm, and I hiss in pain. "You know what? This is exactly why we broke up, Soph. You just lie all the goddamn time, whenever it's convenient for you."

"And you only ever hear what you *want* to hear!" I snap at him, before I can stop myself. "I've tried every which way to explain to you that I can't deal with you like this, Jordan. But maybe the alcohol's killed all the brain cells you use to hold onto long-term memories."

He grabs my other arm, and a surge of fear rushes through me. I know I shouldn't be yelling back, escalating things. I *know* it. But I'm scared, and my mouth is running away with me again, trying to prove I can stand up for myself.

"God, you fucking bitch!" he growls. "You know what? I came here to try and be nice, to try to work things out. But you've just always gotta *dig*." His voice is rising now. He's properly angry. "Every time, *every* time. I try to be nice, and you treat me like shit!"

I can feel the tension ratcheting up again. It's this—this awful, gut-punch feeling—that made me run the first time. His grip is painful. I'm going to have bruises on my arms later. My instincts scream that he's going to lose control and hit me soon.

So I slam my knee between his legs.

I strike paydirt. Jordan chokes on his next words, barely able to speak. I don't waste time—I run past him for the building I've just left, sprinting shamelessly for the door.

I make it inside, my chest heaving. The halls are empty though; there aren't many classes in this timeslot, and everyone who *is* here is taking their exams. Elijah's classroom is almost on the other side of the building; I need to find someone closer, if at all possible. I wrench open doors as I go, searching for one that's unlocked, safely occupied. Most of them don't even open.

But one of them does... and I stare inside, struck by realization.

There's a small class inside with their heads dutifully down, working against a timer. The professor at the front of the class is tall, well-muscled, steel-haired. I just finished her final exam three days ago.

Professor Winslow.

I push my way through the door, ignoring the dirty looks I get from the people still taking their exams. Professor Winslow looks up at me and immediately frowns. Something about my posture or my manner must have set off her instincts, because she strides up to meet me surprisingly quickly.

"Sophie," she says, in a calm, direct voice. "What's going on?"

My mouth opens. Closes. I don't know why, but I suddenly feel frozen to the spot. I *know* the situation is serious. I know I should tell her exactly what's happening. But the last time I tried to explain things to a cop, I got asked if I'd been hit.

I didn't let him hit me. I left again, before he could hit me. I've fucked up, I can't ask for help—

"You're predisposed to avoid asking for help." I remember Elijah's words suddenly. I'm predisposed in more ways than one, I realize. I'm *also* just scared to ask. I'm scared to be told that I'm stupid, that I'm imagining things, that maybe I'm in the wrong.

I could ask to hide in this classroom for the next hour. Professor Winslow would probably let me do that—she'd respect my privacy and not ask why. But I need *help*, god damnit. And at some point, I have to believe that someone is going to back me up.

"My ex is outside," I tell Professor Winslow breathlessly. "He's... drunk. He tried to grab me, and I, uh. Did some damage to him." I wince at the euphemism—but Professor Winslow just looks mildly impressed.

"Good job," she says. "Does he need an ambulance, or a pair of handcuffs?"

I choke on a semi-hysterical laugh. *Oh my god.* I'm being listened to. After more than a year of being talked down to and given the stink eye until I go away, someone halfway-relevant *gives a damn.* "I don't know how bad I hurt him," I admit. "I just ran as fast as I could. But if you know *any* way someone might put him in a jail cell, even just for the night, I'd be so fucking grateful, ma'am. He didn't hit me, but I *know* he was going to, and now he's going to be so *pissed*—"

Professor Winslow pats me fondly on the arm. *Fondly.* God, that's weird. She pulls out her cell phone and starts dialling. "Don't worry about it, sweetheart," she says. "He's drunk on campus and making a scene. At the very least, I can make sure someone puts him in the drunk tank tonight. What's his name?"

I stare at her, not daring to breathe. I give her Jordan's name. Professor Winslow chats almost casually with someone on the other end of the line. None of the students currently working on her exam dare to even look over at us now—the woman in front of me is an authoritative menace. Right now, I can't thank god enough for that.

Professor Winslow snaps the phone closed and looks over at me. "I'm going to head out and look for him, to make sure he's not putting someone in danger," she tells me. "As soon as I leave the room, I want you to lock the door behind me. Don't let anyone open it again until I come back."

I nod numbly and do as she says. Afterward, I sit down in the back row next to the door.

A good ten minutes later, my phone dings. I glance down at it, bewildered. There's a text from Elijah, and I curse myself instantly.

ELIJAH: Are you all right? Where are you?

I can't believe I didn't think to say something to him. I type back quickly.

SOPHIE: I'm fine. I'm in Professor Winslow's classroom.

Far quicker than I expect, there's a hard knock on the door. I jump, but I can hear Elijah's voice on the other side. "Open the door, Sophie," he says.

A few more students glance up. I wince. I know I'm technically not supposed to open the door... but I *also* don't want to leave Elijah outside. I quickly unlock the door and let him in, closing it back behind him and relocking it. Elijah grabs me gently by the shoulders, clearly searching me over for injuries.

"You're not hurt?" he asks, in a low, worried tone.

I shrink back a bit. My face is on fire. I'm aware that he's touching me gingerly like this in front of a whole classroom full of students—some of whom are probably in *his* other classes. "I'm... I'm fine," I assure him. Elijah's fingers brush across one of my arms where Jordan grabbed me though, and I flinch. His face darkens instantly.

"That boy is lucky he's in the back of a cop car," Elijah snaps in a chilly voice.

"He is?" I widen my eyes. Until this moment, I realize, I wasn't truly convinced that Professor Winslow was telling me the truth—that she'd really be able to get Jordan away from me for the whole night.

"He is," Elijah mutters. "I saw the sirens outside. I only managed to get part of the story, and no one seemed to know where you were."

I let out my breath slowly. "I…" I can feel tears threatening, now that I'm allowed to feel relieved. But I force them back and straighten my spine. I can just barely explain away Elijah being here—he's established with Linda that he's taken an interest in my situation—but I know that if I start crying here, there's a real possibility that he'll cross some obvious professional lines. "I'm fine," I repeat, more strongly this time. "I'm supposed to wait here until Professor Winslow returns."

There's another knock on the door, just as I say the words. "It's me," Professor Winslow says. "Please open the door, Sophie."

I let Professor Winslow inside. Her eyes settle instantly on Elijah, who's still hovering over my shoulder. I see a faint crease in her forehead, but she doesn't otherwise comment. "Mister Lynch has been arrested for attempting to get behind the wheel drunk," Professor Winslow informs me. "He's in the process of being booked and charged. If you want to mention his assault, I can show you to someone to get your statement taken— but my honest opinion is that you should go home and relax for the night." She smiles thinly. "As much as I wish it were otherwise, a drunk driving charge is far more serious than what he's provably done to you, and more likely to keep him locked up for an extended period of time."

I let out my breath, dazed. It feels unreal. *Jordan is*

getting locked up, I think. *Even if it's just for now. I don't have to worry about him showing up for the night.*

Elijah shoots Professor Winslow an incredulous look. "You don't think he ought to be charged with assault?" he asks. He sounds faintly outraged. "He laid hands on her! I'm sure he scared her witless!"

Professor Winslow shoots him a dry, withering look. "What I *think* he ought to be charged with and what's more likely to stick are two very different things, Elijah," she says. "Sophie asked me for my help, and I'm doing my best to give it. If she needs an expert in machine learning, instead of advice on the law, I'm sure she knows where to go."

"Thank you," I tell her quickly. "Thank you... *so* much. I really appreciate it, ma'am."

Professor Winslow frowns at me. "I'm glad you came to me," she says. "But I can't help but notice this seems to be an ongoing situation. Why didn't you say something before, Sophie?"

I wince. *Ugh.* In retrospect, it seems so obvious. Why *shouldn't* I go politely ask my ex-cop professor how to handle a difficult legal situation? But I already know why it didn't come to mind. "I guess... I got so used to people telling me there was nothing I could do that I started to believe them." I glance down at my feet uncomfortably. "But also, ma'am... with absolutely all of the respect in the world... you scare the living hell out of me."

One of the nearby students dares to glance over at us. "*Amen,*" he mutters beneath his breath.

"Focus on your test and mind your own business, Mister Espinoza!" Professor Winslow barks at him. He jerks in his seat and ducks his head back toward his exam.

Professor Winslow shoots me a withering smile that suggests she knows exactly how ironic the whole situation is. "So noted," she tells me. She turns back toward us both again. "Well… if it makes you feel any better, I don't foresee Mister Lynch giving you any trouble in the near future. He's not even going to be eligible for bail until tomorrow morning, once he's been fully processed. After that, he's going to have a lot of legal trouble ahead of him. I'll make sure no one in the department is inclined to cut him any unearned slack."

I give her an exhausted, endlessly grateful look. "Ma'am," I tell her. "You are a literal saint. I am going to find you the *biggest* apple for your desk."

Professor Winslow actually *laughs*. It's a small, terse laugh, but I'm fairly sure it's genuine. She reaches into her pocket and pulls out a business card. "Give me a call over break," she says. "I've got some other things I'd like to talk to you about—but I figure those can wait." She pats me firmly on the shoulder. "Have you got a ride home?"

I carefully avoid looking at Elijah. "I do," I say. "Thank you. I think I'm going to take advantage of that right now."

10

ELIJAH

Sophie has been bearing up awfully well for someone in her position. If anything, I'm forced to admit, I'm taking the whole situation far less well than she is. I'd had my own thoughts as to how I might solve Sophie's situation—but it somehow never occurred to me that something might happen before I managed it. I feel like an idiot, overlooking that reality. I can't imagine what I would have done if she hadn't thought so quickly on her feet.

By the time I've found us both something quick to eat and driven us back, Sophie's all but fallen asleep in my car. I hate to wake her up—but even as I try to pick her up, she shifts and blinks awake with a yawn. A silly smile crosses her lips as she looks up at me, and it drives the breath straight from my chest.

"Hey," she says tiredly. "I aced that fucking test, didn't I?"

I choke on a laugh. "I haven't even had a chance to check, you cheeky twit."

Sophie starts pulling herself up out of the car—but I help her up to her feet, holding her against me. I stay there for an extra moment, calming myself down as I feel her heart beat against me.

"...you're a mess," Sophie accuses me.

I shake my head. "My god," I mutter. "And you aren't?"

"I'm *fantastic*." Sophie laughs incredulously. "No one has ever so much as slapped Jordan on the wrist. Now he's in the drunk tank for the night, *and* his father is going to have to drive down to bail him out. I know it's probably going to get even worse as soon as he's sorted out his legal trouble—but I'm going to enjoy being free, just for tonight."

I tighten my arms around her. I hate that this is the extent of her hopes. I want to give her more than that. I sigh as I realize I'm going to spill the news early. "Sophie..." I begin. "I'd *intended* to have a nice, calm conversation with you about this. But I think it's better if you hear it now."

She glances up at me, suddenly wary. I rush on quickly, before she can get too worried. "I know you've only got one semester left here," I tell her. "I'm sure that the last thing you want is to redo a few credits. But I've had an old coworker trying to offer me a job back in London for the last year now. I called him up and asked him if the company might sponsor a permit for one of my research assistants. He just got back to me today."

Sophie's eyes go wide. "You... you're *leaving*?" she squeaks.

I want to shake her in frustration. "I'm *asking* if you want to go somewhere else," I correct her. "If I accept this job offer, they'll hire you as a junior programmer. You can transition to one of the universities in the city to finish out your degree over the next bit."

Sophie blinks a few times. It's a lot to take in, obviously. Even now, I'm starting to second-guess myself, wondering if I should have eased her into it over the holidays. But she sags into my arms in abject relief, clinging to me like a lifeline.

"Oh my god," Sophie whispers. "There'd be a whole ocean between us. Even if he sorts out this drunk driving record, there's no way he's going to hop a plane and track me down in *London*."

"That *was* rather the idea," I inform her dryly. But my heart is pounding, and I know that I desperately wanted her to say yes. The fact that she seems to be favorably disposed toward the idea relieves me too. "To be clear... is that a yes, Sophie?"

She bunches her fingers in my shirt, sucking in a breath. "That's a... it's an *almost certainly?*" she manages. She sounds a little bewildered now. "I've never even been to another country. I mean, I know that's kind of the point, but I'd have to figure out an apartment, and I'm honestly not even sure if I *can* rent something out over there—"

I give up. I press my hands to either side of her face, and I kiss her very soundly, shutting her up.

She kisses me back instantly, throwing her arms around my neck. I like the feel of her in my arms. I know it's something I can't possibly give up. I want to hold her every day for the rest of my life.

Eventually, once I'm quite sure I've kissed all stupid thoughts of rugged American self-sufficiency out of her head, I pull back to catch my breath. "Sophia Eddings," I tell her, "I am asking you to live with me. If that bothers you, then I'm sure we can find some other sort of arrangement. But I must say, I'll be *very* surprised if you'd rather sleep alone in some awful little London flat than let me tie you up in my bed every night."

Sophie shivers against me right on cue, and I know I've successfully used her weak spot once again. She fiddles with my shirt button. "You might get sick of me," she accuses. "What happens in a year, when you decide you want to strangle me?"

"Sophie," I say tiredly, "I *already* want to strangle you. It's part of your charm. But on the off-chance that things don't work out, you'll be gainfully employed, with a very generous starting salary."

Sophie wants to keep arguing. I can *feel* it in her body. She's starting to see the worries, the what-ifs. She's feeling guilty at the idea of accepting a bit of nepotism, no matter how many other perfectly awful, unearned things she's had to deal with already.

But to my surprise, she takes a deep breath... and nods. "Okay," she says. She sounds surprised at herself, too—but she doesn't take the word back. "Okay. That sounds lovely. And I... I *want* to go with you." She summons up some last bit of strength, and looks me in the eyes. "I think you should know that I'm head over heels in love with you. And if that bothers you, then you'd better say so now."

I wasn't expecting to get hit with any more over-the-top surprises tonight... but that one definitely side-blinds me. I have to blink a few times to process it.

You are? I want to ask. *For what mad, hare-brained reason?*

But instead, I open my mouth and say: "I love you too, Sophie. I assume that doesn't bother *you?*"

Her eyes finally fill up with tears for the first time tonight. I don't have long to wonder whether they're good or bad tears, before she's thrown herself into my arms and kissed me again.

Later that night, she falls asleep naked in my arms, and I think again: *I'm in love with this gorgeous, frustrating woman.*

I have the distinct feeling that if she ends up staying in England permanently, it will be with a ring on her finger.

EPILOGUE

SOPHIE

What an absolutely crazy difference a year can make.

It's a terribly busy winter holiday for me—but all of it is good. Linda tells me my landlord has utterly capitulated in short order, given the terrifying legal letters she sent his way. The amount he agrees to pay isn't nearly what she promises she could get in court—but it's sizeable enough that I could replace all of my furniture and pay for an apartment deposit and still have some left over, if I really wanted. As it turns out, though, I don't actually *need* to buy any of those things; instead, I get the news that I've got a British work permit underway, and I need to start the paperwork to switch universities and give my two weeks notice at work.

I have a very pleasant coffee with Professor Winslow, who tells me that Jordan has been sent to court-ordered rehab. It's not prison, exactly—but it definitely means he'll be out of my life for the next few months. With luck, he might even turn his life around and get into a healthier frame of mind... but either way, I'm not going to be here to deal with it. Professor Winslow *does* broach the subject of law enforcement with me—specifically, the sort of federal-level positions that involve money laundering and other computer-related crimes. It *does* put a bug in my head, but I admit to her that it's something I'll have to look into later, once I've gotten my life a little more stable.

Tonight, I head out of my evening class, frowning at the sky. It's drizzling again. Of all the things I've had to adjust to in London, oddly, it's the constant, on-and-off drizzle of rain that's been the hardest to handle. If I'm going to be honest, I *do* find it a little depressing. But the city has plenty of other fantastic things to recommend it —not least of which is my boyfriend, the devastatingly handsome blond who's waiting outside to pick me up and take me home.

Elijah grabs my bag from my shoulder and opens the passenger door of the car for me. "Well, *that's* a unique expression on your face," he observes, as he kisses my nose. "Did you perchance take a bite out of the wrong citrus fruit?"

My lips twitch upward, in spite of my mood. "No," I tell him. "But I think my *professor* might have a lemon permanently wedged up his ass."

Elijah blinks and presses a hand to his chest. "I'm *quite* sure that I don't," he assures me. "Though I suppose you can check if you really need to be sure."

"Not you," I laugh. "I mean my professor from the class I've just come out of. He's so..." I narrow my eyes at him. "...*you.* Except that he's far less charming, I suppose."

Elijah chuckles as he slides into the driver's seat. "As I

recall, you seem to prefer that sort of thing. I don't have competition, do I, Sophie dear?"

I choke on the insinuation. "Oh, *god* no," I manage. "Ew. He's about a hundred years old, I think."

Elijah coughs. "Well, you *do* like older men—"

I hit him in the chest. "Keep talking," I tell him. "It's doing you *worlds* of good."

That smirk of his just keeps inching upward. "You'll only have to deal with one more semester of insufferable British professors," he reminds me. "After that, god willing, you'll be graduated. What *do* you intend to do with your newfound freedom, by the way? Have you any thoughts?"

I let out a breath. "Oh, hell. I think I'm going to focus on work and take a bit of a break, otherwise. It'll be nice not trying to juggle my time so much."

Elijah considers this. Finally, he shakes his head. "No," he says. "I don't think that will do. I was insinuating you might take an *actual* break, Sophie. Perhaps some vacation time. Somewhere a bit less... bleak." He flashes me a smile, and I know he's making fun of me. I've only complained about the rain a *hundred* times by now.

"Ha ha," I mumble. "But actually... that's a good idea. Did you have somewhere in mind already?"

Elijah grabs a small box out of the glove compartment and passes it over to me absently. "I was thinking I've always wanted to honeymoon in Paris," he tells me. "But that might be too cliché. I figured I'd ask your opinion first, since the decision involves you somewhat, as well."

I stare down at the little black box in my hands, wide-eyed. I know what I just heard—but I have to run the words through my mind again, just to make sure I've parsed them correctly.

I open up the little box... and sure enough, there's a ring inside. It's silver wire, set with a small, tasteful ruby. It's exactly the sort of elegant, understated thing I might have picked out for myself, and I know without needing to check that it's perfectly sized for my ring finger. Elijah is just too damned sneaky and cunning to have missed a detail like that.

"So?" he asks me. There's a smirk on his lips again. "Paris? Too tacky?"

I'm glad he hasn't started the car. I throw myself across the space between us, kissing him desperately. Elijah catches me belatedly, and I'm surprised to feel him shaking. As confident as he seems, I can tell he's absolutely dying for an answer.

"*Yes!*" I manage. "I mean—yes to the—I'll marry you!"

Elijah lets out a faint sigh of relief. He holds me close, kissing the top of my head. "I'm sure you'll come around to the Paris idea," he says, forcing himself back into a nonchalant tone. "I can be *very* persuasive."

I grin against him. I'm buzzing with such a wonderful high that I can't even bring myself to argue. "Tie me up tonight, professor," I whisper in his ear, "and we'll see if I *come around.*"

Elijah smirks down at me, and I know it's going to be a *very* good night.

ABOUT THE AUTHOR

Ivy Collins writes short, geeky romances with a hint of spice. She lives in Montreal, Quebec with her fantastic, prose-inspiring husband and her two cats. When not writing romance, she can be found running D&D or Pathfinder for her local group. She is a veteran gamemaster with more than twenty years of experience.

* * *

Want more short, geeky romances? Keep up with my releases when you sign up for my mailing list.

https://ivycollins.com
info@ivycollins.com

ALSO BY IVY COLLINS

Dating & Dragons

Dating & Dragons

A Wicked Encounter

The Paladin Wears Plaid (Forthcoming)

Standalones

Date My Professor